CROSS CANYON

A WYOMING HORROR STORY

D1590151

JN MASTER

ISBN: 979-8-9872033-1-6 (Paperback)
ISBN: 979-8-9872033-0-9 (Ebook)

Printed in the United States of America.

Interior design by FormattedBooks
Edited by Duo Storytelling
Cover art by Sajal Kumar

I would like to thank Jon J. Master;
Clarisa Zacherl; Rob Greene; my NEPA fan club;
my South Pole friends; my beloved wife, Jenna;
and the people of Wyoming, for whom
this story is dedicated to.

Some beauty should not be tread but left
only as a tomb for the ancient dead....

1

CHAPTER

The cold, dry wind raked down the weather-worn and tanned faces of the men driving their small herd of stragglers down from the fall grasses high in the Wyoming plains. The distant, white-crested mountains were lit aflame with the light of the setting November sun, foreboding the oncoming fury of a blizzard. The snow-dappled wind whipped past the three mounted men and across the vastness of the unfinished land.

With a nervous eye on the approaching storm and the other cast upon the back of the cattle now descending into a canyon, Vick, the foreman of the McGregor Cattle Company's cowboys, pulled the collar of his wool coat up as high as it would stretch. The bitter Wyoming wind drove it flat against his shoulders as soon as he released it.

"Damn this all!" he cried out against the whistle of the wind in the grass, not expecting to be heard by either of his two nearby mounted partners.

"*Damn this all* is right!" Carlos agreed, turning his cheek to his own woolen collar and glancing over at Vick. "This seemed like a good idea a few days ago, but now—"

"Yeah, I know. But what do you expect for November? At least the herd has the same idea we do: staying together to get the hell down from these high plains and outta this wind!"

"Out of the wind to be buried by the drifts that are sure to blow in from that blizzard coming straight at us. We'd better get them moving before it gets much darker. It is going to be a long enough night as it is. I can barely see the mountains anymore!"

"If there hadn't been so many of them still out here, they could've stayed here all winter," Vick shouted over the wind, which was now whistling through the reins in their hands. "I guess finding them wasn't such a good thing after all. Let's just get them the hell out of here and back home. Come on, let's get moving. That valley looks a lot better than being up here, freezing to death—drifts or not!"

The two cowboys spurred forward to catch up to Rib, who rode near the back of the herd.

"Guess no one wants to be out in the open with this snow tonight," Rib quipped. He shivered and held his canvas slicker closed. "Too bad they didn't move this well together yesterday. Or the day before that. Or the day before that."

Within a few minutes, the men had dropped out of the wind and into the mouth of the gaping valley. The herd moved effortlessly between the steep sheltered walls, and the men looked around as they trailed closely behind it.

Vick said, "Well, getting them to stop tonight ain't going to be too hard either, with the amount of snow that seems to be headed this way. It looks pretty heavy. We'll need to find a good place to stop and hunker down."

"Where are we anyway?" Rib asked.

"Not exactly sure. We're a long way from anywhere I've been, but if we're where I think, we have to keep heading north. I hope this valley keeps going in that direction, but I don't think it does. Even so, we're still a long, long way from the ranch, and this gap in the high range heads down through a bunch of canyons. We're gonna have to keep going down one way or the other!"

"Great!" Carlos yelled angrily. "So we're going to be out here a while. It's already been a week!"

"Looks that way. We'll go as far as we can before the snow gets too high or it gets too dark. Maybe we'll get lucky and this will miss us, or we will drop below it in the broken country ahead."

The three men took one last look at the snow falling hard on the high mountain plain behind them, hoping Vick's foreman optimism would prove true. But the sting of cold flakes blown through the fiery red rays of the evening sun robbed them of those hopes. With cold, gloved hands and faces tucked deep into their collars and silken scarves, they reined their horses through the sage and onto the worn trail pocked by the hooves of the herd ahead of them.

Evening drew on as the troop of men, horses, and cattle pressed forward along the valley floor, crossing from one side of the dry creek bed to another and back again. They followed an old game trail that had been worn into the pages of history, written out in layers of dirt and stone that rose ever higher above them. They continued through the red-orange rock and sage-covered ground as the trail threaded its way further down from the ravaged high plains above.

After a few miles, the trail began to favor the right bank of a dry creek bed that ran down its center, and their progress became much easier. With the high walls of the deep valley now surrounding them, the men lifted their faces at the sudden absence of the wind.

"Looks like we might get lucky," Vick said, watching the herd continuing miserably ahead of them. "I think we need to start looking for a place to hole up for the night."

"That sounds good to me," replied Rib. "How much farther do you want to drive them tonight?"

"Let's move them a little farther and see if there's better shelter for a camp. We seem to be getting ahead of this storm a bit, and by the looks of things, the further down we go, the better the cover should be."

The men paused to rest for a few moments. The brief calm of the storm was accented by heavy flakes of snow dropping through the last rays of the setting sun. The red scoria rim above them burned with an amber glow against the darkening sky beyond. For a moment, the serenity of it filled each man's heart with a sense of peace and purpose that could only be found amid the bitter extremes of a Wyoming sunset. But such moments are not meant to last, as the sound of the wind above chased the brief reverie from the cowboys' minds. The seriousness of the task at hand rekindled, and they pressed the herd deeper into the valley.

As they moved along, Vick began to take account of their general direction. The last light of the day was quickly absorbed by the thickening snowfall. The valley floor was now dusted with a thin layer of white, mixing with the dirt from the passing hooves of the cattle. Not long after, even those freshly trodden tracks would fill in with snow.

Vick pulled his hat from his head and slapped it against his thigh, knocking a heavy layer of snow from its brim. "With this snow piling up and it getting pretty dark," he called to his charges, "I think we need to push up that next little side canyon for some shelter. If this snow keeps coming down and drifts like it looks like it's going to, we will never get the herd out alive. It looks like that little canyon has an aspen stand at its head, so we should at least get some decent cover for the night."

Carlos and Rib nodded and turned their horses to get around the small band of cattle and divert them off the loose trail. Vick drove the stragglers along from the rear.

Without much effort, the cattle crossed the valley floor and climbed up the opposite bank. They corralled into a small, dry stream bed before the aspens that marked the opening of a tightly walled canyon. Without much choice of where to go and the blizzard now fully dropping down on them, the group made their way around the canyon's head into the small stand of timber. The grove of trees stretched from wall to wall and provided a necessary break from the storm. Much to Vick and his crew's relief, the brunt of the storm seemed to be blocked by the high walls of the canyon, with only the heaviest snowflakes gently filtering down from the raging gale above.

In the waning light, the shapes of snow-covered cattle could be seen slowly plodding through the quiet aspen grove. The freshly whitened ground among the tree trunks gave a half light to the darkening world. Encased in what seemed like a peaceful world of its own, the cowboys rode further on. Not wanting to tempt fate too far beyond its current generous mood, Vick hoped to press on a little farther for a spot that would not be prone to the deep drifts that were sure to flow into the canyon overnight.

With the good fortune of some visibility and calming wind, the band slowly made their way among the aspen grove further up the canyon floor. The dry stream bed began to show traces of ice melt pooling around the scattered stones in its course. In gentle turns to the left and right, the valley pressed on, taking them farther from their course. Every now and then, the trees would give way to a small clearing of tumbled rock from the cliff wall above. A collection of small pines and juniper grew among the rocks near the edges of the valley floor.

The horses' bowed heads and weary strides were beginning to show signs that the snow had deepened and that the band had traveled for too long into the stormy night. Vick reined in his horse toward the others, who were slowly moving up behind the last cow. It was time to make some sort of shelter for the night and hope for the best, come morning.

As Vick wended his way through a small patch of aspen and low brush to reach his fellow cowboys, he noticed that they both had stopped. The herd ahead of them stood still for the first time that day, preparing to make their stand against the coming night. Through the still-falling snow, he spied what appeared to be the widening of the canyon ahead. Vick felt a pang of relief, vindicated for pushing on to find a more favorable spot to camp.

Elated to finally be stopping for the night, Vick caught sight of a freshly made track in the snow ahead of him. He peered down at it from his saddle as he rode by. Its large stride surprised him, and he began to wonder if a mountain lion had snuck out unseen from a hidden pocket of brush. As he tried to reason how he could have missed the creature, Vick dismounted to have a closer look.

The snow was quickly filling the tracks, and Vick struggled to figure out their shape as he led his horse along to find a clearer indentation. A cold bite of fear struck Vick in the heart when he found an unmistakable print pressed into the side of a nearby sage. The track looked human and was headed in the same direction as the men.

"Damn," he muttered to himself.

Vick led his horse through the timber to the other men. Although he was anxious to see if they could explain the footprint, he was leery of mentioning it in case they could not.

Having long given up clearing away the snow from his hat and shoulders, Carlos gazed darkly over to Vick as he approached. "Looks like they found their stopping place for the night. We should be doing the same."

Carlos's unchanged disdain for the situation told Vick that he hadn't seen the maker of the tracks.

"Let's get settled somewhere around here," Vick said.

The thought that someone else was out here in the storm didn't sit well with Vick. From the hasty-looking stride of the track, he suspected there was someone in the canyon that had no intention of meeting them in the open.

Running into someone else in the wilds of Wyoming in the 1880's was sketchy in the best of conditions, but now it seemed even more ominous. After a long pause and another half inch of snow piled on their heads, Carlos grew impatient.

"What the hell's wrong with you?" he growled. "And what the hell do you want us to do, Vick? I would like to get off this horse sometime tonight!"

Snapping back from the weary blur of thoughts he'd been caught up in, Vick begrudgingly announced, "There's someone else here."

"What?" asked Rib, leaning forward in his saddle to see Vick's face more plainly. "What did you just say?"

Given that Vick was not one to lie or even make the remotest attempt at a joke, Rib had reason to fear. Although young and less experienced, Rib had seen his share of the cowboy life—one of hard people and dangerous places. He'd left home a few years back and joined up with Vick and the McGregor Company, finding religion along the way. He loved the beauty and remoteness of the land. It brought him peace and closeness to God.

He'd trusted Vick the day he took him under his wing as a greenhorn. Rib found Vick to be of an honest, good nature, but nonetheless a hard man most of the time. Vick's decisions always seemed to provide more chances for him to ride further into the beautiful, soul-healing land. Rib would follow him through the gates of hell without a second thought.

"I said someone else is up here," Vick answered again. "Keep an eye out. I cut their track just now." He pointed in the direction of where he'd found the footprint.

"How did we not see them?" Rib asked. "I can see the cows from here, and they're farther away! Which direction are they headed?"

Before Vick could respond, Carlos grumbled. "Whoever it is, they didn't know we were coming.

They made the right choice not to stick around and surprise us out here." He reached down and gripped the icy Colt on his belt. "It doesn't matter anyway. We need cover for the night, so let's follow them. This time of year, they ain't staying out in this either!"

"Carlos is right," Vick nodded, looking back at the quickly disappearing tracks. "They're headed up the valley. Let's follow them a ways to see if they have a cabin or something nearby. We'll deal with them when we find them."

Vick turned his horse and led them back to the track, which they then followed along the valley and into the snow-filled darkness. Carlos and Rib kept an eye ahead as Vick picked out the track. Soon, they entered the opening that the cattle had claimed for the night. Their brown coats were covered with heavy, wet snow. Presumably fast asleep in their miserable huddle, none of the herd took notice of the passing men. It appeared they would need no looking after for the night.

As they pressed on in the deepening snow, the tracks grew further apart. It was almost as if whoever left them had been running from something—like a fleeing animal. Vick drew his horse to a stop as the blizzard fully enveloped them again.

Carlos rode up beside him. "Are you sure this ain't no cat?"

Staring intently into the dark, Vick simply spurred his horse forward. "It ain't no cat."

Carlos followed Vick's line of sight to see what had gotten his attention. There, in the deepening gloom, appeared the shape of an unlit cabin.

With Rib bringing up the rear, the three men rode on toward it. As they drew nearer, they could see that it sat near the sharply rising western canyon wall. Although the cabin was in decent condition, no sign of life could be made out in the darkness. The lack of any lantern light from within was unsettling to Rib and Vick, although neither man mentioned a word of this at the time.

Only Carlos, having a much more skeptical view of most situations, made the first rational move to dismount his horse near the cabin entrance. Drawing his Colt revolver, he walked around to the back of the cabin to have a closer look.

Vick also dismounted, handing Rib the reins to his mount. He walked to the heavy wooden door and gave a push. It didn't budge. He kicked the deep snow away from its base to reveal that the door was partially buried by windblown debris.

Vick looked back at Rib, who was searching for some reassurance from his trusted friend. At that moment, Carlos rounded the far corner of the cabin, completing his circuitous inspection.

"Find anything?" Vick asked.

"Nope. No light, no other doors, no fire, no more tracks, no people. Nothing. Where's your cat now?" Carlos sneered at him.

"Well, maybe it was. Nobody has been through this door for a while." Vick didn't want to believe he'd misidentified the footprint, but he couldn't make sense of why a person wouldn't shelter here in a storm like this.

"Well, I don't know where they're heading, nor do I give a damn," Carlos said. "But I know where we're sleeping for the next few days by the looks of it. And it ain't gonna be in the snow!" He strode past Vick and kicked the door off its rotten-leather hinges and onto the wooden cabin floor inside.

"Nice one, Carlos," Rib drawled. "We might have wanted that to keep the cold out."

"Just shut up, kid!" exclaimed Carlos, stepping through the door. He dusted the snow off his clothing. "It smells like shit in here anyway!"

Rib quickly dismounted his horse and stepped through the low doorway to escape the blizzard's cold. "Shit? Smells more like something died in here."

Ignoring the terrible smell and the mystery tracks for the moment, Vick got back to making sure they would get through the blizzard. "Rib, find something to burn and get a fire going. Carlos, prop the damn door back up after it airs out a bit in here. It could use some fresh air, but we ain't gonna be able to build no fire without that door standing up. I'm gonna get our bedrolls and bags off the horses, then picket them up for the night out in those trees in front of the cabin. If the door was bigger, we could just bring 'em in."

"Maybe Carlos can work on kicking a bigger opening into the front of the cabin to get them in here," jabbed Rib, feeling less apprehensive upon hearing the confidence in his foreman's voice. The three men shared a much-needed laugh.

The mood eased as Vick barked orders as though it were any other night of bad weather. As the work went on, they even began to feel that they might pass the night in comfort compared to the previous days on the trail. The cabin was a lucky find. They would be tucked neatly out of the howling blizzard outside.

Rib found an old lantern with some fuel hanging from a peg on a center post above the cabin's table. With light in hand, he searched for wood for the fire. He was elated to find a small, dust-covered pile of pine stacked neatly in a corner near the rough stone hearth. Within minutes, they had a nice blaze going in the old fireplace, despite the breezy open doorway.

Returning from the blizzard outside, Vick carefully piled up their essential gear to dry in front of the roaring fire. He warmed his hands next to the blaze as snow melted from his coat, steaming in the fire's light.

"Going to leave their saddles on them tonight," Vick said. "The temperature is really dropping, and they're already miserable. It might keep them a little warmer out there. Rib, I'm setting your rifle by the fireplace here. Gonna need some oil after this ride."

Vick propped the lever-action rifle in the corner beside the mantle. He took his own Colt from its holster and removed the cylinder to make sure the barrel wasn't packed with snow. The thought of having a run-in with the mystery person out in the storm was not wholly out of his mind. He was certain they weren't far away.

"Best have you oil mine too when we get back," he added as he wiped the pistol on his sleeve and slipped it back into his belt. "Carlos, get the door!"

Carlos sat up from the chair he'd pulled to the fireside and walked over to prop the door into its frame. With the support of a nearby chair and a good deal of sand piled on the cabin floor, the door was secure enough to keep the wind out and the warm air inside.

Before long, the cabin began to feel comfortable in the dancing firelight. After pulling up chairs to the fireplace, the men began to root through their packs. Soon, a meal of hardtack and elk jerky was passed around. As they sat among their steaming coats, hats, and gloves, the mood lightened.

After much talk about what they would do once the storm passed, the conversation inevitably turned back to the set of tracks that they had followed.

"You really think those were people tracks, Vick?" asked Rib as he poured coffee into Vick's blue-enameled tin cup.

"Yeah, I do. Somebody is out there, not far away," said Vick, holding the hot cup under his bearded face. He breathed in the comforting aroma. "They had to have seen us, and they probably won't miss this fire in here either."

They all sat quietly for a moment.

"Which makes me think that we're going to take turns watching that damn door tonight," Vick said grimly. He looked to the only window in the cabin, thankful that the glass was still intact. "Hard to believe it's still in one piece since the rest of this place is a mess. Unless you saw another way in here, Carlos, that door is the only entrance. You looked around in here with that lantern, right?"

"That's the only way in I saw besides the window," replied Carlos, who hadn't bothered to examine the cabin's interior much beyond the table in the center.

"Good," reaffirmed Vick.

Rib topped off Carlos's cup of coffee before pouring his own as he scanned the room. "You think it's a Cheyenne or someone just passing through to get out of the weather?" He watched nervously for Vick's response, not paying attention to the scalding rim of his cup. It burned his lip, and he yelped and spilled it on his lap. "Dammit, that stings!" He leaped from his chair amid the rolling laughter of the other two men.

"Boy, that oughta warm you up quick," Carlos jeered. "If that works, let me know!"

Gathering his composure, Vick smiled and said, "I don't know who laid those tracks out there, but I hope they didn't want any of Rib's coffee!"

While Rib stood in front of the fire to pull his coffee-soaked trousers away from his already-soaking-wet legs, Vick circled back to Rib's question. "I really don't know who it is, and I guess I don't really care at this point. I'm only sure that whoever they are, they're no good in any case."

Carlos, seeing a chance to play on the young man's fears, took a small sip of coffee and said, "I'm pretty sure this is the cabin those lost homesteaders from a few years back must have built. Guess we solved that mystery—they came to a bad end after all."

"Are you kidding me?" Rib's eyes widened.

Vick answered before Carlos could reply. "No, he's not. The story of the homesteaders is true. I was thinking the same thing. In fact, years ago, I went out with one of the parties to try to find them after they went missing. They bought a few head and some supplies from McGregor's and headed out this way with their little family to settle. Everyone figured they were killed in an Indian raid. When we couldn't find no sign of them, we figured that they'd just kept heading west. No one ever knew. By the looks of it, this is where they ended up."

They pondered the fate of the family for a moment, silent in the firelight.

"I'm not entirely sure where we are," Vick went on, "but I think we're coming through the badlands farther out than we intended. We never looked for them this far out."

"Well, I'm sure this is where they ended up. I found this on the table." Carlos pulled a tattered leather-bound book from his coat on the chair beside him.

"What the hell is that?" Rib croaked.

Vick simply lowered the cup from his lips and stared at the little brown book.

"It's one of their diaries, I think," Carlos said. "The daughter's, I'd guess, from the handwriting on the front pages. Haven't read any of it yet, and pretty sure I don't want to until we're the hell away from here."

The three men felt a tinge of fear in their bones as they stared quietly at the diary, although none of them admitted it.

"Why didn't you tell us about it sooner?" Rib finally asked.

Vulnerability and fear—feelings Carlos hated and tried to hide beneath his grim exterior—swept over him as he held the book in his hand. They reminded him of a painful time in his youth when he was weak and afraid of those that would hurt him. As though caught in a trance, unable to escape these feelings, he sensed that something was focusing hatred upon him as he examined the book in his hand.

"Would you have wanted to know?" he snapped suddenly. "Would you feel better, Rib, knowing you're holed up in some homesteaders' cabin where God-only-knows-what happened? You can barely keep from bawling your eyes out about whoever's out-side, let alone being snowed inside this godforsaken cabin in the middle of nowhere!"

"That's enough!" Vick barked, snapping out of his own uneasiness. "Now, we're not going to worry about it, and we sure as hell aren't getting spooked enough to start tearing each other apart! We're going to have a long night out here, maybe even a couple, so cool the shit, boys! Like it or not, we're stuck in here for now, and we don't need no ghost stories making it worse. Rib, sit down and drink that coffee before you toss it all over yourself again!"

Carlos held the diary silently a few seconds lon-ger, then set it on the hearth. As he did, a shrill wind screeched through the braced doorway. They turned to look just as another hard gust burst down the chim-ney and threw sparks at their feet from the crackling logs. They all looked at each other in the firelight for some strength against their growing fears.

Carlos broke the silence first. "You know, this book is the only thing I found in here that didn't have any dust on it."

"We're trying not to get spooked about being stuck in here, Carlos!" Vick scolded, trying to regain some of his authority as foreman. "How about you keep things like that to yourself for the night? I'm just going to say it. Whoever is out there probably has something to do with no one being in here. But there are three of us and one of them."

Carlos went on as though he hadn't heard Vick speak. "Not even the Indians come into the canyons out this way, if we're where you think we are." He tapped his foot nervously against the floorboards and shook his head. "We should have left the damn cows. Nobody comes out here!"

"I think Rib is good and scared enough as it is without you adding to it, Carlos. Now shut up!" Vick thought for a moment. "It changes nothing. We still need to weather this blizzard. At least we're lucky enough to be doing it with a roof over our heads and a fire keeping us warm. And yes, if you must know, I wish we hadn't come out this far either. Hell, we have a long way back to the ranch, even if we end up leaving the cattle behind. But chances are, we'll be glad we have them. Looks like we'll be holed up here awhile by the sounds of that storm out there. I've seen this before, boys, and it could be spring before we can get outta here. I rolled the dice. I'm not sorry about it. So, let's get this whole thing outta our minds now!"

The other two men sank in their chairs at the admission from their foreman.

Seeing the disparaging looks on their faces, Vick went on. "But we're not going to be up here forever. We're going to make it back down, with or without those cows. We're going to do our jobs and get out of here as soon as we can."

Having had enough of the conversation, Vick rose from his chair and threw a few more logs into the fire. "Rib, you take first watch here by the fire. Wake someone up if you start to get tired. If the door wasn't braced, I'd check on the horses, but there ain't much we can do for them tonight, anyway. They should all be good, and they certainly aren't going to wander off. We have plenty of wood for a day or two and can worry about finding more if we need it. Anyway, kill that lantern back there for the night. We should save the oil for when we really need it. Keep it handy though. Now, good night, boys. We had a long day, and I'm thankful that we're tucked in here, no matter who's fool enough to be running around out there. See you in the morning."

The three exhausted men turned their minds away from their solemn discussion and organized themselves in front of the fire for the night. Vick and Carlos situated themselves on the floor in front of the hearth, using their saddle bags to keep their heads out of the dirt. Rib pulled his chair nearer to the wood pile and gathered his rifle into his lap to start his watch. As he did, he tried not to obsess over the miserable thoughts stalking his young mind. He hoped desperately that the morning might find the blizzard gone and the trail home open.

As Vick was pulling his wool blanket up around his neck, he peered over his shoulder and said, "Rib, don't forget the lantern."

Rib snapped out of a longing stare into the coals of the freshly stoked fire and stepped carefully between the bedrolled men. After extinguishing the light, Rib turned a wary eye over his shoulder to the blackness beyond the window in the back of the cabin.

With the darkness and firelight now dancing their eerie waltz among the old timbers, the deep shadows outside seemed to stare inward with a horrible delight. Feeling a sudden chill, Rib turned away before his mind could fall prey to the trickery the glass played upon his eyes. He returned to his chair and rifle, near the beckoning warmth of the hearth.

As the wind of the storm moaned its lonely song down the canyon, the night drew into a weary dream of darkness.

Just beyond the window, a shadow broke from its vigil over the men inside its lair.

2

CHAPTER

With a violent heave of his body, Rib woke to an inconceivable stillness. He struggled to remember where he was, and the silence began to grip him hard. He could hear his heart pounding as he took stock of the situation. He wondered whether he was really awake at all. The darkness of the cabin seemed to envelop him in a world with no direction or substance.

As he scanned the ever-thickening shadow, his eyes caught sight of a few embers still smoldering in the hearth. The storm outside had fallen silent sometime in the night. Deadly silent.

Now with some small bearing on his surroundings, he remembered where he was. The paranoia that had consumed him before he'd drifted off began to slowly return. Rib slid back into his chair and pulled his rifle closer as his eyes adjusted to the darkness. Feeling the encroaching cold biting against his uncovered neck and shoulders, he expected to see the door cast from its frame or pushed aside, but it appeared to be in the same state as the last time he'd checked—God only knew how many hours ago that was. Holding his breath and looking toward the back wall, his fears eased a bit when he saw the window-pane was still intact.

Loosening his grip on his rifle, he dared to take a deep breath again. The heavy breathing of Vick and Carlos in their nearby bundles assured him that all was well.

Still holding the lever action, Rib picked up a log from the stack and carefully pushed the embers into a pile. Within a minute or two, the thread of thickening smoke burst into a flame that climbed up the dry pine logs Rib carefully stacked around it.

Having regained his composure, Rib decided he was no longer tired. He would continue the watch to allow the others their peaceful slumbers. As he sat there, he marveled at how both Vick and Carlos could sleep in such uncomfortable positions, though he was also a bit jealous of the skill. He consoled himself that it was simply something that one perfects when one gets old. He was content to not share in this art of misery for the time being.

Rib chewed on a piece of jerky that he drew from his pocket as he added a few more logs. Staring into the fire and feeling the room warm around him again, he noticed the snow drifts beyond the window were now softly visible.

Sitting up, he looked toward the door again and at the dim light coming from the world outside through the gap along the frame.

"The moon is out," Rib muttered.

"What is it?" Vick grumbled to Rib's surprise. He rolled from one shoulder to the other and pulled his blanket back up around his ears.

"The moon is out, so the snow must have stopped."

"Good," said Vick. "Have you heard anything out there?"

"Like someone outside? No."

"That too, but I meant maybe the horses or the herd stirring. It seems pretty calm, and I don't hear them."

Rib sighed in relief. "No, but I can go and have a look if you want. It's pretty light out now with the moon."

"Sure, it wouldn't hurt, I guess. Pile a couple more logs and be quick. I bet it's still cold out there." Vick rolled back into his warm bedroll.

Happy to have something to do, Rib tended the fire so it would blaze a bit stronger before he prepared to have a look around. He tucked his gold cross, a gift from his mother, back into his undershirt and tied his now-dry and now-warmed silk bandana around his neck. With rifle and hat returned to his person, he carefully stepped over his companions, who both stirred and searched for another chance to fall back asleep in front of the rising fire.

Rib carefully lifted the door and placed it on one side of the open frame. The aspens outside were now visible across a small opening that he hadn't seen through the piling snow some hours before. The moonlight on the snow and canyon walls drew softly into his eyes, and the bite of winter's deep chill met all his senses at once. He stepped through the doorway into the knee-deep snow.

He felt a peacefulness in the crisp wilderness night that he hadn't had since before the misery of the day. It was just a few hours before dawn, based on the stars now happily visible in the cobalt sky above the canyon walls. Rocks and small trees on the far canyon wall descended into the wide stand of moonlight-flecked forest in front of him. Deep shadows wrapped around the tree trunks like a cloud of impenetrable night against the fresh blanket of deep snow. The opening in which the herd had come to rest seemed bright and inviting under its open canopy of stars, but he couldn't hear them or detect any movement.

With the moon lighting his way, Rib trudged in that direction through the deep snow. The going was slow and exhausting, and after what seemed like an eternity of lifting his knees to his chest, he arrived at the edge of the glade. The herd was nowhere to be found.

"Dammit!" he puffed, and the vapor of his breath blew into the cold night air. Dusting the snow from the action of his rifle and turning back toward the cabin, he began to retrace his broken trail and attempted to find their horses in the timber nearby.

He pondered what might have happened to the herd. How would the company ever get them out of there with all that snow, and how long would they be stuck there because of it?

Rib turned from his track and made his way into the shadow of the trees where Vick had left the horses. The wood seemed to draw in around him as he fumbled forward. The cabin flickered in and out of view to his left, looking almost beautiful and inviting in the moonlight, despite the bitter cold.

That was to be the last sense of peace that Rib would know in his very short and unfortunate life.

Rib was suddenly struck with horror and came to an abrupt halt. His eyes strained to see through the steam of his quickened breath. He was too terrified to make a sound at what he saw before him.

The lifeless bodies of their horses were hanging from the branches of a large aspen tree. Tears of fright and sorrow welled in his eyes and froze midway down his cheeks. What sort of savagery could have done this—and without them hearing? Each horse had been torn open and lifted into the branches by something with unimaginable strength. They were tethered to one another and strung up by their reins, their open wounds still steaming in the cold night air. Blood soaked the deep snow below them and marked their trail to the base of the tree.

Numb with fear, Rib turned back toward the cabin. His eyes darted all around, searching for the beast that had killed the horses. Before he knew it, he'd stumbled into a large trail broken in the snow.

Droplets of blood shone along the trail in the moonlight. Freshly cut in the deep, wet snow was the same footprint they had been tracking before. It was easy to see that it was of great size and clearly human. An unholy feeling gripped Rib as his eyes traced the trail out of the trees to the open door of the cabin.

No sooner had Rib's gaze reached the open cabin door than Vick's yells rang out and were quickly silenced. A gunshot pierced the night, followed by a shrill, unearthly scream that reverberated off the walls of the canyon before tapering off to a distant echo.

The once-beautiful night seemed to become shrouded in a haze of sickness as Rib stood immobile in fear, listening to the cries of the struggling men inside fighting for their lives. Finally, drawing the courage he had left and knowing there was no chance for his friends inside the cabin, Rib gripped his rifle tightly and began to run.

He stopped abruptly, as if he'd forgotten something. Not daring to look back, he pulled the cross from beneath his shirt and tore it from his neck with a sharp yank. He pulled his right hand from its glove and wrapped the chain so tightly around it that it drew blood as he pressed the crucifix into his palm. He resumed the run through the piled snow as fast as his panic-stricken heart would take him—away from this scene of horror and back down the canyon floor.

Trying to remain out of sight of the cabin, Rib quickly broke through the edge of the cattle glade, into the aspen stand where Vick had first seen the track. Stopping only briefly at the last faint scream of one of the men in the cabin, Rib tried to hold back his sorrow and guilt over leaving his friends to their horrible fate. Selfishly, he thought their apparent deaths might just give him the chance to escape the beast he heard languishing in their tortuous murders.

Standing there, in the shadows of the timber, Rib's resolve gave way to uncontrollable sobs, and he fell into the snow. Putting his hands over his mouth to muffle his whimpers, Rib pulled himself together enough to stand and press on.

He'd managed to escape the view of the cabin. Weariness from scrambling through the snow and stumbling over buried fallen trees began to set in, and Rib felt exhaustion taking its toll. Despite this, he continued to press on.

After what felt like hours of trying to get as far from the cabin as he could, the bitter predawn cold began to find its way into his sweat-soaked layers. He stopped to catch his breath and finally looked back in the direction of the cabin. Nothing could be seen following him through the plumes of his breath, nor were there any more of the terrifying sounds.

He began to move painstakingly through the deep snow of the timber bottom, the moon painting the walls of the canyon in soft light. Some hope of survival sparked amid his fear and exhaustion, as time and distance now seemed to be on his side.

Just as suddenly as hope entered Rib's mind, it was ripped from him once more. Rising from the forest not far behind him, a half-animal, half-human voice screeched the words, "Death comes for the child!"

He stopped and spun, searching the shadows for the beast he had hoped would not come for him.

With his spirit broken and body shaking with fear, Rib knew his end was drawing near. Dismay overtook him as he fell against an aspen tree and sat at its base. There were no more tears to shed, nor the energy to shed them. The silence that he'd once so desperately sought now haunted him. The moisture of each exhausted breath began to freeze to the scant amount of beard he'd managed to grow. He watched the woods along his backtrail, waiting for his inevitable end.

It didn't take long. Light snow began to drift into the canyon, bringing the promise of another storm that would march across the dawn, now not far away.

A gentle breeze blew from the woods that he now watched intently, and with it came the rotten smell of death and the warm scent of fresh blood. It drifted over him like a heavy fog. A dark shape stepped into view, searching the trail Rib had left.

With his last shreds of courage, Rib leveled his gun over his knee and pointed it at the darkened being. The moonlight illuminated its tattered cloak, and he realized it was much larger than any man or beast he'd ever seen.

At the movement of his rifle, the creature, only a dozen yards away, stopped and stared him down. Rib felt it feeding off his fear as his heart pounded in his chest. It seemed to grow larger, as if all the shadows of the night were being drawn into it.

Slowly, the creature began to hunker down into the broken trail, as if it were preparing to leap at the terrified man.

Rib glanced at the beloved cross still held in his right hand. Feeling no longer alone, he was ready for the end. He gripped the crucifix so tightly that blood dripped onto the snow beside his leg, and his fear began to fall away. The beast roared as if it felt Rib's fear turn to courage and faith.

Rib looked down the barrel of the rifle and centered the rifle in the middle of the beast's head. Its roar was more demonic than beastly, and so loud that it seemed to rend the very walls of the canyon. The beast's clenched, jagged teeth glinted faintly as it sprang upon him.

Rib closed his eyes and pulled the trigger.

3

CHAPTER

The war had been long. When he found that everyone and everything he'd known as a young man had changed after his return, life no longer made sense. The world had turned upside down, partly from the changing times and partly from the demons inside him—demons that would never leave.

Staring through the dusty windshield of an old Bronco, as the soft rays of the westering sun painted the grassy plain rolling out before him, Steven felt little peace. His family, his friends—all gone. He'd spent too many years being a good soldier, never anything else. Too many tours. Too many people that didn't understand him when he returned. Too many years of a broken life.

For all the things he'd done during the war, the way his nation had cast out the returning soldiers seemed like a bitter, unjust penance. He was happy that most didn't make it home to see what awaited them. They weren't thought of as the heroes they all once boasted about being, but as baby-killers and murderers. Every young soldier's dream to rise above poverty and be hailed as a hero of their hometown was spat on by the very friends and loved ones they'd grown up with. Yet these people hadn't been out there, so how could they understand? Steven and the rest had been sent without a choice, their dreams broken and twisted, with luck as their only ticket home from a jungle far away. The boys who'd left home had returned as broken men.

The beauty pouring through his windshield snapped Steven out of his reverie. The decision to pack up and leave the crowded East Coast was the right one, a comfort he'd long searched for.

Hours of listening to the Bronco's tires whir down the highway had stretched into days. Wyoming was a familiar sight that recalled his time long before the army. He'd come here with his father and uncle to hunt and fish when time and money had allowed it. It was among his fondest memories.

Stiff from the road, Steven pulled off the highway and into a gas station on the outskirts of a small town. He stepped out of his 4x4 with a stretch and a deep breath of the cool fall air.

Not seeing any attendant nearby, he flipped on the pump and started refilling. A moment later, a shock of white hair appeared from behind the counter on the other side of the station window.

Having been caught dozing, the old man inside jumped to his feet and pulled on a greasy jacket before making his way out to the pumps. The bell above the door jangled behind him.

"I could have got that for ya," the attendant said, tugging his jacket closed against the cold.

Steven didn't feel like having a conversation with another stranger who would wonder what he was up to in a vehicle with Pennsylvania plates. He simply looked at the approaching attendant with the usual measure of distaste that he had for everyone.

"Here, I'll finish that up for you," said the attendant, stepping between him and the pump handle politely. "So, you on your way to go hunting?" He looked at the army jacket Steven still wore proudly over his broad shoulders. The old man leaned around the back of the dusty Bronco and quickly peered at the out-of-state plate.

"No," Steven replied, scanning the distant mountains across the plain and small town ahead, trying to avoid conversation with an old man who obviously had nothing better to do.

"Oh, just passing through then." It was more of a statement than a question. A painfully awkward silence hung in the air as the old man started to scan the same horizon. The slow pump trickled gasoline, cent by cent into the nearly empty tank.

Steven glanced at the old man. He probably lived for the stories of his passing customers. In a rare moment of pity, Steven offered a reply. "I'm looking to move out here from back east," cutting right to the chase.

The old man's eyes lit up. He turned toward Steven and unleashed his carefully planned questions for such occasions. "That's a long ways from home to be coming out here. Must be quite a change."

"A little. Not too much of a home back there, so I thought I would give it a try out here."

"Yeah, probably a good place to get away these days." The attendant chuckled. "My son was back east for a little while and didn't care for the people much. It just seems to be falling apart everywhere now. At least, there aren't too many people out here for you to run into. The wind keeps them away," stated the old man proudly with another chuckle and having gained a better sense of the man that stood before him.

Feeling a little better about offering up information about himself, Steven added, "I came out here as a kid to hunt with my father and uncle."

"Whereabouts did you and your family go hunting back then?"

"Up in that range over there, I believe. Don't remember exactly. I forgot how big Wyoming is. But I know we weren't too far from this town."

Jumping forward through his usual line of questions, happy to have the stranger from Pennsylvania now talking to him, the old man said, "I imagine you did pretty good hunting up there. Not many folks hunt in that area. It is still a pretty good place." Without waiting for a response, he moved on to his next series of questions. "So, where are you looking to move to?

In town here? Not much of a town, but a good place to get away. Not sure who might have a place for ya, but I'm sure something could be arranged for a young fellow like yourself." His eyes scanned Steven's Airborne Ranger and Delta patches. "Unless, of course, you're heading farther down the road?"

Steven chuckled at the barrage of questions. "I am really not sure, I guess. Is there a motel in town where I could get a room for a night? Getting tired of sleeping in this old truck. I remember an old blue place my dad liked to stay at before we went up into the mountains. They had a nice little diner next door." As he spoke, Steven's mind flooded with warm memories of the diner and people as kind as the old man standing next to him.

"Well, if you were looking at those mountains over there and stayed in a blue motel with a diner next door, that could only have been here in town." The old man laughed. "That would be the Ranger Motel."

"That was it!" blurted Steven, with an excitement he hadn't heard in his own voice in years. "Is it just down the main street, here?"

"Yessir! Ms. Jill still works there too. It's her place and her diner. She'll be happy to have you, I'm sure."

The old man pulled the nozzle out of the Bronco's tank and returned it to the old pump.

"Well, I do appreciate you helping me sort that out." Steven smiled and handed the attendant a wad of cash. "It was good talking with you."

Steven opened the driver's-side door, then paused to look at the mountains in the distance. "If I were to stick around for a few days to go check out the mountains again, I'd need some supplies. Maybe you could point me in the right direction when I come to fill up again. This thing likes to eat the gas." He laughed. It felt good to have had a conversation with someone after so long.

"Certainly can help you with that." The old man smiled and politely closed Steven's door behind him.

Steven fired up the old Bronco. Before taking off, he leaned out the driver's-side window and said to the old man still standing nearby, "Did your boy get himself out of all that mess happening back east?"

"Yeah, he did," the old man answered. Pain laced his voice and pride filled his eyes. "Right out of the east and into that war. The army called him up, and he never came home." He patted Steven firmly on the shoulder. "Glad you made it, son. To here, I mean. Go down and see Ms. Jill. She'll get you set up and find you something to eat."

The old man looked at the mountains, then reached through the window to offer a handshake, which Steven gladly accepted.

"Thank you, sir," said Steven. They met each other's gaze, quietly understanding the loss they each carried.

Steven turned the Bronco onto the main street and headed toward the motel. The sun was in his eyes, so he adjusted his visor. Thinking back on the old man's words, he remembered why he'd come here: to try to escape the demons and nightmares that followed him.

As he pulled in beneath the blue neon sign of the Ranger Motel, Steven couldn't help but smile. If the rest of the people in this town were as true and welcoming as the old man, his journey to start anew may have already been over.

4

CHAPTER

Steven was up with the dawn. The old, cozy motel room hadn't changed a bit since he'd stayed there as a kid. Each detail was exactly as he remembered.

With a stretch, he paused in front of the dingy mirror above the tiny bathroom sink. The man he saw before him reminded him of his father, who had stood in front of this very same mirror so many years ago.

The wood panel of the room in the reflection still bore the same paintings of elk and deer as when Steven, his father, and his uncle had crammed into this double-twin bedroom. Steven remembered looking at them, excited for the coming day's hunt, as the two men finished their morning bathroom rituals. The drive from Pennsylvania had been especially long, but this had been a favorite hunting area of the Millson family for generations. Although they'd gotten in late the night before, Steven had been dressed and ready hours before the other two and waited as patiently as a twelve-year-old could for his first exploration of the mountains.

He recalled his father, smiling at him in the mirror as he shaved, asking, "You excited, Steven?"

The night let loose a flood of memories, from the worn red carpet to the smell of Ms. Jill's menthols permeating the room to the cool Wyoming air drifting from the office. It was nice to find that some things hadn't changed, even things that had flashed by in his youth.

After spreading his gear out on the empty bed, Steven traded his proud army jacket for his grandfather's old Woolrich coat. He straightened the collar in the mirror by the tiny sink. It was not the first time this mirror had seen that coat, he recalled.

The old screen door creaked as Steven stepped out to the concrete motel porch and into the brisk morning air. He stood in front of the Bronco, rooting for his keys. The smell of bacon and eggs from the diner next door caught his attention. Once more, he was overcome with pleasant memories.

In uncommon fashion, he was beginning to feel relaxed. He placed his keys in his pocket and walked past the empty rooms of the motel and toward the diner.

The first streaks of sunlight were welcome on Steven's face. The clean, pure morning seemed to hit him all at once, and he paused to enjoy the moment. He listened to the sound of distant birds and a small creek in the nearby cottonwoods. Just outside of town, cattle called out to a passing ranch truck as it left a cloud of dust in its wake. The mountains lay darkly in their morning shadows beyond that, framed by a sea of grasses painted with pinks and reds. Blue mists rose in the first light of the day. Everything seemed to be locked in stillness by the cool air.

Feeling more like the kid he once was and less like the man who woke up struggling against every day, he continued across the dirt parking lot lined with idling livestock trucks.

Passing between a row of ranch pickups parked neatly along the front of the diner, Steven noted how even the diner hadn't changed. It still bore its clean, metallic lunch-car exterior. Many cowboy hats were perched in the window frames beside their dining owners. A small thread of steam rose into the cool air from a vent on the roof, sending the irresistible smell of breakfast into the Wyoming breeze.

As he climbed the weathered concrete steps to the entrance, Steven noticed the glow of the fresh morning sun reflecting off the polished steel façade.

Coming back to the moment, he began to feel a small measure of apprehension as he passed through the first set of double glass doors into the vestibule that shielded patrons from the harsh Wyoming wind. It had been a long time since he willingly placed himself among so many strangers. As he reached for the second set of glass doors, many of the people inside glanced at the newcomer they had spotted crossing the parking lot.

Despite his apprehension, he pushed on into the crowded eatery. The brass doorbell announced his entrance overhead. A thin smile spread across his lips as yet another memory was evoked by the ringing. Steven scanned for an empty seat among the booths and stools. Photos of cattle drives and rodeo cowboys filled every inch of wall space. All of them had faded in the sunshine that poured through the front windows. The inside, warmed by the grill and the dozens of dining patrons, smelled as marvelous as the outside.

As Steven hung his jacket on the nearly full coat rack, he was greeted with a loud "Good morning!" from the old man from the gas station, who was seated with a few old men several booths away.

Gathering his bearings among a sea of staring patrons, Steven headed to the tall unoccupied stools adjacent to the old man and his friends. It seemed to be on the somewhat quieter end of the room, yet all eyes were on him as he crossed the diner.

It was apparent that most of the town's population started their days at Jill's. Once he'd settled, the patrons of the diner turned back to their own conversations, seemingly happy to have a new face to share in the daily ritual of breakfast. The drone of patrons laughing and talking among themselves began to rise once again.

"So, did you get some good sleep?" the old man from the gas station asked. "Looked like you were the only one pulled into the motel for the night."

"I did," said Steven, as he turned to the waitress now standing before him. It was Jill's granddaughter—also named Jill, according to the nametag. Steven asked for a coffee and some of the bacon and eggs that had drawn him in, then turned back to the men. "I haven't had that good a sleep in quite a while. Better than sleeping in that truck, for sure!"

"I figured that you were made of some tough stuff. Takes a man to sleep in his truck all that way. Not many of those around anymore!"

Steven laughed along with the men and a few busy-bodies who were listening in on their conversation.

Breakfast moved along in the normal fashion for a small-town Wyoming restaurant. Small talk and discussions of the day's ranch work and cattle moving. Clanging silverware. A busy waitress with a coffee-pot suspended over the heads of patrons crowded in booths set the scene in the morning light pouring in through the front windows. Everyone was polite to one another; the gentlemen removed their hats while they ate and extended old-time courtesy to the ladies who got up from their tables.

Curious folks sitting nearby asked Steven a few friendly questions, and he was happy to answer them while trying to finish his meal and another cup of coffee.

People began to filter out to attend to their daily business. With many a wave goodbye and a few handshakes between the local ranchers and their ranch hands, they dusted off their cowboy hats and slowly filtered out to start the day's work. Steven began to feel pretty good about his choice to stick around for another day.

The old man and his friends stood up and pulled on their worn ranch coats and tattered winter hats. One turned to Steven with an earnest expression.

"So, will we be seeing you here for dinner tonight?"

"Yessir," stated Steven happily. "I'm hoping to go and get a look around those mountains today. Going to take a drive there this afternoon."

"Stop by the little general store before you turn off the old highway. You gotta make your turn up into the range anyway, and you'll need to fill up. Old Joe here won't go under if you get your gas there."

They all laughed.

"They'll have about everything you might need. It belongs to Young Jill's mom and dad—Bob's place." The old man smiled over the counter at the waitress, who was caught staring at Steven with a smile of her own.

"Her mom is Jill's daughter," noted one of the other old men, casting the remark down the diner at the older Jill working on the register. "They have it all sewn up around here!"

"I never got your name, son," said Old Joe from the gas station, thrusting a hand forward. "I'm Joe."

"Steven," Steven replied, standing and gripping Joe's hand in heartfelt return. It was nice to have someone finally care to ask for once. Joe's friends went around with similar introductions, happy to have met Steven as well.

Steven put on his coat to follow the party of old-timers out the door. He stopped and turned toward both Jills with a smile. "Should I be asking for Jill, Bob's wife, at the general store?"

Both laughing hardily, the younger Jill replied, "No, her name is Clarisa!"

Now in an even better mood, Steven stopped by the office to tell the clerk he would be staying a few more days. Then, keys in hand and eager to begin looking for more old memories and the chance at making some new ones, he opened the Bronco and tried firing it up.

He bought the trusty old vehicle before he'd left for Special Forces training and his third tour in Vietnam. The hand choke needed some coaxing, seemingly developing contempt for the higher Wyoming altitude and persistently colder temperatures. But, true to form, it didn't let the army vet down, and he turned it over on the second key turn.

As he pulled away from the parking lot, he felt good enough to cast a wave to Jill and Jill, who were watching him from inside the diner. He was certain they were discussing him. He was the new talk of the town, after all.

Steven slowly made his way between the small brick buildings of Main Street, taking account of all the storefronts—some of them still housing businesses, others empty. A few ranch pickups and a couple of cars were parked here and there, with even fewer people coming or going. Of those few, many immediately recognized Steven and his out-of-state

Bronco from the diner. All cast him a big wave as he passed. Even the sheriff gave a happy wave over the roof of his pickup as Steven drove by the steps of the courthouse.

Word of his arrival apparently had traveled fast, as had the townsfolks' acceptance. The sheriff hadn't been at the diner that morning yet waved at Steven like an old acquaintance. Steven found himself grinning as he pulled away from the other end of Main Street, which was marked by a set of old railroad tracks. He felt very unlike his normal angry self.

It was obvious that life there had bustled more prominently once upon a time. The rusty remains of an old railcar and industrial equipment bordered an old railyard that was lined with grain bins. Signs for jobs that were no longer around clung to the rusted bins, giving reason for children to leave a good home like this.

At the edge of the tracks, an old sign displaying a population of 307 marked the town. Steven wondered how accurate that number was.

Pleasantly distracted by the events of the morning and wondering whether Young Jill was single, Steven began to pick up speed in accordance with the posted speed limit.

In short order, he was bathing in the strong morning light that beamed across the plains around him. Steven enjoyed the heat on his face as the airy cab began to warm. He couldn't help but admire the cattle-dotted ranches that seemed to stretch to the very base of the mountains beyond. He thought about how the world was waking up in the shadows of the high peaks, now softly glowing with the promise of a new day—a day that seemed to confirm his hope that this could be where he would find peace. It was what he secretly hoped for since the war and the hell that had followed him home.

The journey from a boyhood spent hunting the woods and fields of Pennsylvania and the mountains of Wyoming to manhood was a short one. Like many poor boys of his time, there were two choices once high school was over: willingly join the army in the hopes that you might choose what you do in Vietnam, or let the government draft you and send you there anyway. The day high school ended, Steven had enlisted and headed to basic.

Back then, it was not a war without end but one with an inevitable, glorious American victory against the evils of communism. People at home were proud to know a soldier. Practically everyone he knew—including his grandfather, father, and uncle—had been soldiers, fighting for freedom around the world. The choice to be a soldier and do his part seemed like the right one. It was in his blood, and he became the best of them all.

However, all that idealism got lost somewhere along the way as the tours went on and he continued to train. By the time he joined the Special Forces, he struggled to see himself in the killer he'd become. The cause no longer mattered as much as the body count and the safety of the men who fought alongside him. There was nothing else. Just the terrible destruction that came so naturally at his hands.

For Steven, there was no returning to childhood innocence. He lost his high school sweetheart when she could no longer fill the hole that grew inside him between tours. While he was home, part of him just wanted to go back and fight, and the other part just wanted to escape the growing vitriol cast upon him by a nation of ingrates who had cheered him into battle only years before.

Alcohol had become the balm to ease that pain. It kept him going. It helped drive away all those that might have helped, and they soon passed away. In the end, when there was no more war to fight, the contempt he felt for everyone, including himself, kept him from going to his own father's funeral.

He convinced himself that he was a soldier and nothing else. He knew it had become his excuse for not wanting to reenter the world around him. In time, he beat the demon of alcoholism and tried to make a new life for himself, but the anger and fear of the people he met pushed him further away from that goal.

A normal life didn't seem to exist for him anymore, no matter where he went. Besides, how could the hands of a killer ever be anything but that? He'd felt his enemies' lives taken by his own hands so easily, and now everyone he saw was his enemy. He hated that he couldn't fit in. He felt more like a villain than a hero, and he despised the coward inside him for not being able to stop it.

After many years, Steven had just accepted who he was and that there were no more enemies to hunt, just enemies to avoid in the States. No one wanted to employ someone with the kind of skills he had, and with an ever-growing distaste for people who would quickly pass judgment, he'd finally turned his thoughts west.

He had nothing to show for his troubled life in the east, but one good breakfast and some friendly townsfolk had finally given him some hope. As he kept following the road out of town, Steven felt as though the fond memories of his childhood were a final gift from his father and uncle, guiding his way home at last.

After a few dozen miles of tires whining on the pavement, he finally turned into Bob's Place, which was just off the old highway.

Steven stepped out with a final morning stretch and walked up onto the wood-planked porch and through the screen door into the small store. Mounts of various game animals hung proudly near the ceiling, where space would allow for the towering antlers. The smell of a good cigar wafted from somewhere deep in the back of the store, overpowering the scent of old wood flooring and the smoked deli meats that sat behind the glass.

Alerted by the creaking wood floors, Steven could hear someone pushing a chair back in an attached room filled with sporting goods and supplies. A man emerged from around the corner, a cigar burned almost to the butt still clenched in his teeth.

"You must be Bob," Steven said.

"Yes," the man answered in surprise.

"And your wife must be Clarisa."

Bob gnawed the end of his cigar and cast an eye upon Steven. "And you must have had breakfast at the diner." Both men laughed. "So, what can I help you with?" Bob moved past the meat case toward the register.

"I'd like to fill up out there and was going to see about getting a few sandwiches."

"I can help you with both of those. First, let's get you filled up."

Crossing the wooden porch outside, the two men made their way to the parked Bronco. As Bob started the pump, he asked where Steven was headed.

With a finger pointed at the mountains, Steven explained his brief boyhood history and how he was going up there to have a look around again.

As they stood there, waiting for yet another slow pump to fill the large tank, Bob pointed out a few sights that Steven might want to visit. He also added some tips for negotiating the tiny dirt road into the mountains not far past the store.

"You should be fine with this buggy and tires," Bob said, taking a quick look around the vehicle. He removed the cigar from his teeth and placed the smoldering tobacco on top of the still-churning pump, then knelt down to have a look underneath. "Good clearance. You'll need it for picking your way up the canyon just over the river. You should be fine, and the road gets better the further you go." He put the cigar back into his mouth.

With the Bronco's tank filled, the two men went back into the store to collect the sandwiches.

"So, you going up for the night or just the day?" Bob asked.

"Just the day. Going to see how far I can get. Hope I make it into the mountains with enough light left to have a good look around."

"You will. Are you staying back in town then?"

"Yes," Steven replied, with no need to elaborate. The Ranger Motel was the only option. "Maybe for a few days." He debated asking some of the questions that had started to build in his mind as he drove the long miles out to the general store. "You wouldn't happen to know of anybody needing some help around here, would you?"

"Oh, those old-timers at the diner would undoubtedly have some work for you. Or they would know who does. They spend more time in that diner nowadays than they do back at their ranches. Their wives are thankful!" Bob laughed. "There's plenty of work around for someone like you with the grit and brawn to do it. A lot of cattle and not many people wanting to do that kind of work."

"That doesn't sound too bad," Steven replied. "I'll have to talk to them about it."

After placing his wrapped sandwiches in a paper bag and squaring his bill with Bob, Steven thanked him and bid him farewell. He hopped into the fueled Bronco, headed down the highway a short distance, and turned sharply onto a small track of road, kicking up dust as he rumbled over the cattle guard.

Steven rode past antelope as the road rolled through the dry, grassy hollows of the plain. The startled animals burst into action, running senselessly to cross the road in front of him. He passed countless cattle grazing, who stopped to stare in his direction as he sped past.

After an hour or two of endless dirt road, he reached the river. Although he crossed it cautiously, the water still rose to his doorframe. Steven began to slowly pick his way up a rough road on the far side. More of a ditch made by melting snow and rain in the earlier part of the year. When he finally crested the top of the washed-out section, the grade of the road settled into a wide, smooth hillside, as Bob had foretold.

Enjoying the warm pine and sage-scented air, Steven had a long-awaited and uneventful day traveling along the mountain road. He got out to eat his sandwiches on the hood of the truck, hearing nothing but a few distant birds, the soft breeze rustling through the woods, and a distant stream tumbling over rocks in the valley below.

Time slipped away as he began to remember what it was like to love being somewhere again. The memories of his uncle and father, of hunting elk and deer in these mountains, had begun to come back.

He recalled getting out of the truck, probably on this same road, in the early dawn. He remembered treading across the soft floor of pine needles, following his father, a rifle in hand. Thinking about climbing up through the steep ridges above, he remembered his excitement as his uncle stopped to listen to a distant bull elk bugling in the dawn light. It was the first time that he'd ever heard anything like it, and he was glad that he hadn't forgotten it. He remembered napping in the hot afternoon sun somewhere on the high slopes above, listening to the mountain breezes as they blew gently through the aromatic pine forests. He felt as though his father and uncle were still up there somewhere in the heights around him. He liked to think that they were watching him from above and seeing how happy Steven finally was for this long overdue homecoming.

As emotionless as he'd become as a man, he was surprised to find himself kneeling in the dirt of the road alongside the Bronco, staining the ground with tears that fell from his cheeks. He didn't hurry to get up, wanting to stay in those memories with the people he loved.

After some more time silently roaming the mountains in his mind, he rose to his feet. Steven took in one more deep breath of the mountain air and climbed back into the Bronco. He didn't wipe away the tears.

As the sun dipped below the high peaks framed by the head of the dark timber valley ahead, Steven turned the vehicle back down the mountain road toward town. Rounding a bend, he was stunned by the beauty of the plain that stretched into the evening light before him. Mountain shadows reached toward another distant range miles across the hazy vastness. And there in the middle, like a beacon, sat the little town.

With a mind now filled with thoughts of another chance to talk with the townsfolk over a good meal, he began to feel as though his darkness would finally meet its end in this magical place. He made his way back down the mountain valley as the shadows lengthened and cooled the air. Crossing the river once more, he drifted in thought as he drove on. Dreams of returning to this high valley filled his mind, as the dust flew out of the Bronco's tracks in the rear-view mirror.

Steven arrived in town after dusk and returned to the motel for a shower and fresh clothing. Fresh linens were set neatly on his bed. Beside them was a note that read "Job: Pearson Ranch" along with some rough directions.

It seemed the kind people of the town were inviting him to stay at least a little longer.

After a quick shower, Steven headed across the parking lot to Jill's diner. He found his new friends at their same spot preparing for their evening meal. Steven pulled up the stool that Jill's now reserved for him at the community table, and he began to exchange the details of his day with the familiar characters from that morning.

Feeling better than he had in years, Steven finished dinner early to turn in for the evening. A diner full of smiling faces bid him good night as he paid his bill and went out into the night air.

5

CHAPTER

Steven returned to his room and, feeling welcomed and satisfied, drifted off to sleep.

The following day found Steven in much the same routine as the one before. His written directions, the likes of which everyone seemed to be aware of, were amended with various tips from the old men and both Jills over breakfast. It seemed that the Pearsons were a good sort of people and would be expecting him to stop by to discuss some work. They might even have a place on the property for a prospective new hand to bunk, if he desired to stay.

A few hours later he was on his way out of town, heading in the direction of the Pearsons' ranch. Passing through the downtown section, Steven was met with the same welcome procession of smiling faces and countless waves. The local sheriff waved as the Bronco hummed by the courthouse. Looking in his rearview, Steven saw the sheriff hurriedly moving toward his patrol vehicle, handling his morning coffee carefully to keep it from spilling as he entered his truck.

After a few minutes of daydreaming amid the sound of tires humming along the highway, Steven looked down at the directions lying on the passenger seat. The diners had warned him of a tricky turn coming up. Glancing back into his rearview mirror, Steven saw the sheriff following closely behind him. When the sheriff noticed Steven's glance, he flashed his patrol lights.

Not knowing what to expect or whether he'd broken the unusually slow speed limit of twenty-five miles per hour, Steven pulled to the side of the road.

The sheriff hopped out of his truck and approached the window of the Bronco, which Steven had already rolled down.

"Not to worry, son," the sheriff started before Steven could ask what was going on. "Jill asked me to lead you out to the Pearson's. Seems you've made a good impression on the folks in town, and they all wanted to make sure you found the turn and didn't keep driving away." He laughed.

Steven chuckled in relief. "Sounds good," he said, looking back at the old sheriff and his stained white cowboy hat.

"Looks like you come prepared." The sheriff grinned, nodding at the large knife being used as a paperweight for the directions on the passenger seat.

"Yeah, sorry about that. I probably should have that in the glove box."

"It is fine right where it is. Looks like it has a job to do there, holding down those papers," replied the sheriff. "This Wyoming wind will blow away any-thing that's not bolted down, but it keeps all the city folks from staying too long."

Steven looked at the knife and the countless notches carved into the handle. "It's definitely a bet-ter job than it's had in the past."

"A good knife is like a good dog. I had one like it myself when I was in the army. Looks like good luck to me," said the sheriff.

"It certainly has been."

Quickly moving away from the subject of the knife, the sheriff jokingly rolled his eyes. "Anyway, I'm heading that way, so you can follow me to the Pearsons' gate. I'm sure you could have found it just fine since you found your way to Wyoming on your own. But since I don't want to lose my booth at the diner, I figure I better do as the Jills ask!" Both men had another laugh, and the sheriff walked back to his truck, shouting over his shoulder, "Follow me, son."

As the sheriff pulled around the Bronco, Steven saw him talking into his radio, undoubtedly reporting back to his office to assure everyone there that he was following his strict orders from the townsfolk.

In a few miles, after making the turn Steven would have surely missed, the sheriff waved his hand out of his window in the direction of a ranch gate with the name Pearson welded on it.

The Bronco rumbled over the cattle guard and down another dusty Wyoming lane, passing small patches of sagebrush and brown grass waving peacefully in the wind. Meadowlarks could be heard here and there, scattered among dots of cattle spread out over the rolling earth.

Steven crested a small rise and crossed another cattle guard. It was framed by a barbed-wire fence that stretched to the horizon on either side. The homestead came into view, sitting neatly in the hidden cottonwood bottom along a creek.

Some wild turkeys ran off to either side of the road as Steven approached. A pair of dogs ran up to meet the Bronco on its way to the house, which was situated near some corrals on the opposite side of the creek.

Slowing to a crawl to avoid running over the dogs now trotting carelessly alongside him, Steven stopped the truck in front of the house. The miles of road ended abruptly ahead of him.

A well-statured, white-haired man stepped onto the porch. The two dogs finally seemed satisfied with their duty of announcing the newcomer and ran to the old man's side. The man dusted off his felt hat and placed it on his head, then strode down the steps to meet Steven.

"Jim Pearson," he said with a hand thrust forward in greeting.

"Steven Millson," Steven replied, stepping out of the Bronco and returning the handshake.

"Heard you might be looking for some work and a place to stay."

"Yes, sir."

"How do you feel about cattle?"

"Don't know much about them."

"That's no problem. The work is hard, and the days are long, but it doesn't seem like that'd be much of an issue for you. Why don't we have a walk around and see how this might work out?"

After being denied work so many times because prospective employers saw the flag on his field jacket, it felt good to be talking about a job again. "That would be great."

After an hour of talking about duties, a tour of the corrals, and an introduction to some of the herd penned inside, Steven felt good about the possibility of feeding, wrangling, and branding cattle. He truly began to like the idea of this new life after being introduced by name to some of the ranch's horses. It seemed like the kind of place he could start again. The work seemed good, as did Mr. Pearson.

As the men walked and talked, Steven gazed out across the vast plain the homestead was nestled into. Here and there, brown dots of cattle in the distance grazed upon the gently rolling terrain. Meadowlarks could be heard calling from the grass unseen beyond the corrals, along with many other songbirds preparing their roosts for the night. The cackling flock of turkeys was making its way up into the roosting tree for the night, just beyond one of the old timber-sided garages near the creek.

Steven hadn't realized that Mr. Pearson's tale of building the thirty-year-old stable had stopped abruptly. They'd been walking in silence, Steven smiling dreamily. Steven quickly apologized.

"Nonsense! It looked like you were somewhere far away without any troubles there for a minute. Wasn't about to interrupt that."

"Yessir, I guess I was! I don't get back there too often."

"Whereabout would that be? Must have been somewhere that had some turkeys, I'm guessing."

"I was just thinking about the last time I saw a flock of turkeys flying up into their roost. It was back in Pennsylvania. My family had a farm there, and I used to hunt the turkeys when I wasn't helping out in the fall. Seeing these birds just reminded me of how exciting it was just to see them. Back when holding a gun and stalking around the woods was a fun thing. Funny how things change."

"Yeah, that they do. Getting older will do that," said Mr. Pearson. "I'm sure you've had your share of holding guns, by the look of it. Won't have much need of that around here, especially since those are Mrs. Pearson's 'wild' turkeys. She gives me fits every time I even think about putting one of them on the table."

Both men laughed.

"So, I'm suspecting the war took you away from the farm, but before it did, what kinds of stock and crops did you grow?"

"I was pretty young when we lost the farm—maybe ten years old. We mostly grew corn and hay and tried to keep a few dairy cows. My grandfather had worked the land as a dairy farm, and my uncle and father tried to keep it going after he passed away. But as stubborn as those two were, it just wasn't paying anymore, and they eventually lost it. It was a pretty rough time for everyone in the family. Especially my mom."

"Pennsylvanians are good folk. Hard workin'. I don't think that I ever met one that didn't love to hunt and fish. My kind of people," said Mr. Pearson, working the conversation away from the negative tone it seemed to be heading toward. He could see a good man in Steven, a man that needed a new beginning. "You mentioned coming out this way to hunt with your father and uncle. I wouldn't be surprised if we'd all sat elbow to elbow, once upon a time, in Jill's diner!"

Thinking about how little things had changed from what he remembered, Steven agreed, and they both laughed again.

After a few more stories, good and bad, the two men found themselves with an understanding of one another. They knew they could rely on each other, there in the middle of the rolling valley the Pearsons had called home for generations.

The hours had turned toward evening when they walked back to the house and stood alongside the Bronco. Mr. Pearson politely demanded that Steven stay for dinner; the missus had already begun to set the table for Steven. She'd made his favorite meal, which they'd been told about by an unidentified source in town. At this, Steven and Mr. Pearson laughed.

"Looks like you're well looked after here already!" said Mr. Pearson as they walked toward the house.

The two men climbed the dusty wooden steps onto the timber porch of the ranch house. Mr. Pearson swung open the heavy front door as he wiped his feet on the mat. He invited Steven inside with a wave of his hand.

Upon stepping through the door, Steven was greeted with the pleasant surroundings of an old log-style ranch house, adorned with many family photos and old paintings. The home felt comfortable and was accented by the delicious smell of dinner coming from the kitchen. A large wooden table stood centered in the adjacent dining room.

As the men removed their coats and hung them on pegs next to a large river-stone hearth, Mrs. Pearson emerged briefly from the kitchen and rounded the table to come greet them. Her introduction to Steven was accompanied by a passing kiss on his cheek. Mr. Pearson asked if she needed any help with dinner, but she just smiled and disappeared back into the kitchen.

As she passed through the doorway, she remarked, "Make sure to wash up, my fellas."

Mr. Pearson placed his hat on the pegboard and led Steven to the old washroom. Steven found himself feeling at home as they passed another wall of family photos in the hallway. The pleasant smell of countless years of smoked beef and wood fires emanated from the smooth planking of the walls and floor.

After a good washing of his face and hands, Steven felt refreshed. Walking back down the hall to the large table, he could hear that Mr. Pearson had joined Mrs. Pearson in the kitchen. As he waited awkwardly for the couple to return, he circled the table and looked around the contents of the room. As he did, he again began to sort through old memories once more of his childhood life with his family back on the Pennsylvania farm.

Soon, he was joined by a freshly washed Mr. Pearson, who issued a warm invitation to pick a spot at the table.

Upon her return to the room, Mrs. Pearson politely refused Steven's attempt to help set the table. When the last of the fare was placed before them, the blessing was given by Mr. Pearson. Steven hadn't heard someone say grace since he was a boy. As Mr. Pearson spoke it, for a moment he felt the peace that he so desperately wanted. After all the kindness shown to him by the genuine people that he'd met over the last few days, he knew that he'd indeed, finally, come home.

Dinner was an ample serving of his favorite dish, steak and potatoes, which was consumed among good conversation. Mr. Pearson retold some of Steven's tales to Mrs. Pearson while they ate. The couple asked Steven a few questions that hadn't come up earlier, and Steven began to open up with questions of his own. The ranch and its family history fascinated him.

"So, when did your family arrive here again?" Steven asked, wiping his mouth after the last bites of his third helping, which Mrs. Pearson demanded he take.

"It was back when Wyoming was still a territory, and they wanted to call the state Lincoln," Mr. Pearson proudly replied. "My great-grandad came here from the east to find work and found my great-grandmother along the way. They settled here with a small herd of beef and began to grow the operation from there. They were the first family to settle here. It was a wild country back then, you can bet!"

"Now, that's not true, Jim," injected Mrs. Pearson. "There was one other family that placed a stake out here before that."

"Yes, that's right, Mother. But my family was the first to make a living off the land here, and the town soon followed them. Glad it never got any bigger than it is," sighed Mr. Pearson as he pushed his clean plate away.

"Yes, my dear," she said, smiling from across the table. "I'm going to clean up dinner and get some dessert. Now you both relax and talk some more without me." Both men stood as she left the table, then sat back down once she entered the kitchen.

"My darling is right as always," said Mr. Pearson as he watched his beloved wife leave the room. Steven couldn't help but smile at the politeness and genuineness of the couple. "There was a family that had tried to make a homestead out here several years before my granddad. A couple and their children, they say. Not much is known about them. Just that they came this way and were never seen again. Somewhere up in the broken step canyons just west of the big range you said you had driven up into yesterday. Somewhere up there is a place they call Cross Canyon now."

Intrigued, Steven leaned forward to listen intently to the story as Mr. Pearson went on.

"It got its name from a cross necklace that was found hanging on an old game trail at the head of one of those big box canyons out there. Too rough a country to ranch and too far out for any sane person to ride into and be able to get back home in a day or two."

"Did that family leave the cross necklace there?" Steven asked.

"No, that cross belonged to a young fellow on a cattle drive that disappeared from the McGregor ranch. It's thought that he left it as a trail marker when he and a couple of fellas that he was with were moving a herd back down out the high plains beyond. They headed up late in the season to find them before the snows came in, and it buried them up there. The McGregor ranch sat about a hundred miles east of here, down along the big river. Those boys didn't make it back to the ranch that fall and were thought to be coming down through a pass way over to the east of where the necklace was found. The snow finally came in, so they must have lost their way moving the cattle down through those rough canyons. The ranch went looking for them but couldn't find a trace. It wasn't until years later that that cross was found by an Indian guide who got turned around leading some prospectors. He brought back some news of the cross, and people knew that it belonged to the boy that was riding with the lost cowboys. That old Indian left it there since it was a place his people didn't like being. He said it was Big Medicine that man should leave be. And he would not have known about that cross, so it must have been where they died that winter. That happened a lot back then. My grandmother had more than a few tales of my granddad and some of his hands spending the winter holed up between here and the summer range from big snows. No wonder she hated him!" Mr. Pearson laughed.

"Sounds like a good place to stay away from," replied Steven. "What did the guide mean when he said that it was Big Medicine and that Cross Canyon should be left alone?"

Mr. Pearson leaned over the table with a look toward the kitchen door. Just beyond, Mrs. Pearson could be heard singing happily as she attended to her after-dinner tasks. "The missus doesn't like me telling these ghost stories, but here goes. The Indian fella was referring to an incident that I heard about a few times over the years from different people when I was young. The tribes that lived nearby tried to warn people about the legends of that area, especially the ones about when things first started to get settled here. I'm so old that I still remember some of those folks passing by the ranch here from their lands somewhere out on the other side of the high range in the fall. They were still trying to hunt as a living, but that didn't last long once we all got here. Good people. Damn shame that they're all gone now. Nobody knew this country like they did."

"That's fascinating," Steven said. "It must have been something to see the last of those people."

"It truly was." Mr. Pearson was solemn. "Anyway, I better stay on track with one story at a time. If I remember it right, that legend was about a tribe that found themselves caught in a bad winter storm out there. It was either in or near what became known as Cross Canyon. Not really sure, but it does not matter. They were trying to get to the low country late in the year, like people do, and a big snow blew in and trapped them. That would have been difficult enough, but it was what followed next that put the fear of that place into the tribes and made it one of their legends."

Steven couldn't help but be drawn completely into this amazing tale of the Old West. He sat with elbows on the heavy wooden table. The fire in the hearth crackled from time to time, adding its own sentences to the intrigue of this tale unfolding before him. These were his favorite kind of stories, with cowboys and Indian legends. To be hearing one firsthand as the lonely coyotes howled outside across the plains was a real treat.

"I can't pronounce the Indians' word for it," Mr. Pearson continued. "But they said it was a spirit of some kind, and not a good one. They said that it came in the deepest most desperate part of that winter and began to prey on that poor stranded tribe. Just like a big mountain lion, it started by taking their children in the night at first. Try as they may, there was nothing they could do to stop it, even though some of them were great warriors. Those nights of terror went, and the snow just kept piling up, making their escape as dangerous as staying there to face that demon. At least that is what I would call it."

"That is quite a legend!" Steven remarked, leaning back into the spindles of his chair.

"Oh, it goes on! That poor tribe's suffering kept on through the winter, it was told. The demon kept taking people, and they started to go mad with hunger and sorrow. Then, one bitterly cold night, she walked right into the middle of their shelters. I say 'she' because it seems that the spirit had taken over the body of one of the teenage girls of the village, the chief's daughter. And she came for him as the village slept. Hearing his missing daughter's voice calling for him, he ran from his tent to find her. And there she was, standing in the moonlight, alive and beautiful. The warriors in the village began to gather to the scene now, too, and couldn't believe their eyes either. But the folks who told us the story, and I've heard the same from a few others, kept mentioning her eyes. Something about her eyes. They said that they weren't the girl's eyes, but those of the evil spirit. Yellow like a cat's. Pretty spooky stuff."

"I would say!" remarked Steven.

"But the chief knew that this was not his daughter, and enraged by what this beast must have done to her, he shot an arrow into her heart. They say she just stood there, as though it did nothing. And that was when she killed them all. They tell of the warriors fighting hard to stop her, but the girl turned into some kind of giant beast and tore them to pieces. After it was over, she dragged off a few men and killed them slowly, so the remaining villagers could hear their cries. It seemed that evil spirit had come not out of hunger like an animal would, but to prey on their fears. And fear they did. Once it showed that it couldn't be stopped and could take anything that it wanted, all those in the village still alive and hiding in their tents lived in terror as they were slowly taken, night after night. In the end, a few escaped through the deep snow and cold.

"The Indians who told us that story around this very table really didn't like talking about it, even though it was just a legend. I guess that they thought we might think they were crazy. They said that it was told as a warning to stay out of that country, but even they were a little skeptical about how true it was. They said that the old ones had a lot of stories like that, and they thought that some of them were just to keep them from getting lost out there. Which is easy enough to do anyway, even without a scary story like that.

"Their story had a bit of a happy ending, I guess, as the tribes eventually got their revenge. The medicine men passed the legend down through many generations so that it would not be forgotten. As they did, they plotted their revenge and awaited their moment. They had somehow learned that spirit was immortal or something and needed people to stay alive. Does seem like more of a scary story to keep youngsters from wandering, now that I'm saying it aloud.

Anyway, the medicine men figured out that the spirit couldn't go far from that country, so they made it a forbidden sacred place. They learned that without people to prey on, that evil spirit grew weaker as time went on, trapped in the chief's daughter's body. So, after many generations passed with no more trouble from her, the tribes joined together and went back into that unholy land. They found her weak inside her lair and buried her alive in it forever. And as those Indians told us, that's why the old ones wanted people to know about their legend. So that she would remain buried in that forbidden land forever."

Pausing to gather his breath, Mr. Pearson leaned back into his chair and looked over at Steven contently. He chuckled.

"Whether you choose to believe that tale or not is up to you. I've been told many ghost stories like that over the years, and I don't believe most of them. But that is definitely one I think about still when I'm out riding home after dark. It scared the heck outta me as a kid. Still does sometimes. Can't help but wonder if those lost cowboys and that family got tangled up with something like that up there. Guess we'll never know—and kinda glad not to!"

"That's quite the tale," Steven said. "Thanks for telling it to me. Back when my dad and uncle brought me, I had no idea anything like that had happened out here. Even if some of it's only a legend."

"It would be hard to know if you didn't live here your whole life. And nobody likes to talk about things like that most of the time. Nobody believes stories like that anymore anyway. Country like Cross Canyon is still a place nobody goes. It's just too rough out there, like I was saying, and there are quicker ways to get around the high range than going out that way. No roads, no trails, and very little water out there for anything. Pretty-looking country to see from afar, but that's close enough for most."

Having caught the end of her husband's tale through the kitchen door, Mrs. Pearson reentered the room with a handful of pie plates and silverware. She rolled her eyes at Mr. Pearson.

"Is he telling that story again?" she asked.

"The missus here doesn't like to hear about all those kinds of things," Mr. Pearson said, smirking as though he hadn't already shared this fact with Steven before. "She thinks it's lonely and dark enough out here at night with the coyotes."

"I told you, if you keep telling that story, I'm moving back to Cheyenne where you found me!"

At that threat, Mr. Pearson's stories began to turn toward his rodeo days up and down the Front Range during the years before he took his turn at running the family ranch. Those stories then drifted into meeting his beloved wife and raising children together.

The coyotes were howling outside, and the sun began to paint its reddened shadows across the plains. Content to telling his stories to a good listener, Mr. Pearson got up and began to stoke the smoldering wood embers in the hearth next to the table.

"You're welcome to bunk in the little creek house by the corral tonight, if you don't want to drive back into town. You can call that home if you want to come back and help out around here," Mr. Pearson stated, making sure Steven knew the job was his for the taking.

"I should probably get back into town for tonight, but I will take you up on that offer, sir. Thank you."

"That sounds wonderful!" Mrs. Pearson exclaimed, peeking in from the kitchen door.

With another strong handshake to seal their deal and a parting kiss on the cheek from Mrs. Pearson, Steven made his way back to the Bronco, stopping to pat the dogs on the porch.

The dust trail cast its long shadow behind the vehicle, out across the cottonwood bottom, and over the rise beyond. Steven was lost in pleasant thought as the night closed in on his ride back to town. Bright stars appeared above the range in the cool distance. Steven pulled back into the motel, went into his small room, and began to pack up his meager belongings for his move to the Pearsons' ranch the next day.

Another note lay on the pillow. This one invited him to the small bar and grill out by the highway. It seemed that a few of the locals would be having an evening drink and playing cards there. It was signed by Young Jill.

Although tired and generally disinterested in anything that might remind him of his past life, this invitation seemed harmless enough. Besides, it was Saturday night. He placed his gear in the Bronco to be prepared for an early start the next day, then hopped in and headed toward the highway side of town.

The small tavern was framed by two small neon lights and a parking lot full of ranch trucks. The sheriff's vehicle was there as well. Steven smiled at the friendliness of this close-knit community. Laughter, conversation, and jukebox tunes buzzed from inside the heavy front door.

Upon entering the bar, the faces of half the patrons lit up with smiles, including Young Jill's. This warmed Steven, melting away his apprehensions. A flood of invitations to sit at various tables poured forth from the town folks as he headed toward Jill. Most people he saw were familiar from town. The ones who weren't all welcomed him as if he'd been a fixture of the community for years.

After many a thank-you and more handshakes, Steven finally sat down at the table next to Jill and some of her young ranching friends. She'd been saving him the seat all night in hopes that he would arrive.

Steven was inundated with pats on the shoulder and anecdotes from the older bar patrons as the conversation moved around him. He strained to hear them talk over the jukebox, which got turned up over the course of the evening. There were curious questions about how things went out at the Pearson ranch and the possibility of his staying around. His agreement seemed to cause a rise of celebrations at the nearby tables. As some folks played cards and others converged on the worn-out pool table, Steven politely sipped his one and only drink of the night and answered questions about himself. The patrons seemed to respect his abstaining from the drinks being brought to the table. They didn't even seem bothered by his quietness among so many new and unfamiliar faces. It was plain to see that he was happy to be there with them all.

Steven volunteered to refill the table's pitcher and bowl of chips. Most seemed to have kept their distance to not intrude at the younger people's table. Jill appreciated this, as she was quickly growing fond of Steven. Good men her age were hard to find in those parts. There weren't many left.

The sheriff and his table of friends had the most questions regarding Steven's visit to Pearson's ranch and seemed most pleased at his decision to stay.

"Had you stay for dinner too?" they asked. "The old man must like you! We put in a good word for you to help you along the way with Mrs. Pearson."

When Steven returned to Jill's table, she was smiling.

"I am so sorry that they're like this. You're the biggest news here in a long time, and they really like you! Usually, they're happy to see people pass through, but once you have the old folks on your side, you aren't going to get anywhere fast. I'm happy you decided to stay too."

In the whirlwind of being swept off a road lined with pain and misery, Steven couldn't remember the last time he was this happy.

But pain and misery were soon to follow him from that same road.

6

CHAPTER

They were a self-proclaimed gang of troublesome bikers. Mostly hardened ex-cons mixed with Vietnam vets. Unlike Steven, however, they had no intention of trying to mend the damage the war had caused them. Their cowardliness was masked by their dangerous ways and disregard for anyone but themselves. They haunted the lost and lonely roads of Wyoming's oil fields, bringing a storm of ill fortune upon the towns set in the lonely in-between spaces.

The cheerful laughter and conversations in the bar subsided at the sound of their drunken clamor and motorcycles rumbling into the parking lot. Many patrons cast worried eyes upon the sheriff as he pushed his chair back from his game of cards and walked over to the side of the bar. A few conversations began to murmur back to life as they awaited the trouble about to walk through the front door.

Steven sensed the fear in the group and in Jill sitting next to him.

"We've had problems with these guys before," she said. "Kinda hoped they would never come back."

One of them explained how this group of bikers had destroyed the barroom a year or so ago, giving some ranch hands broken bones before the state troopers had arrived in force.

Then the first of the bikers emerged through the door.

There were seven men in total, most sporting long beards and muscular, tattoo-covered frames. Half of them headed to the already-occupied pool table. The rest pushed their way past the seated townsfolk to the bar, all while belligerently cursing and mumbling about the lack of room in the establishment and the country music playing on the jukebox.

The loudest member of the gang—their leader, apparently—strode straight to where the shaking bartender stood as the last song ended. He gave no acknowledgment to the sheriff as he walked past him. The room fell deathly silent as he leaned on the bar and stared down the bartender.

Steven began to sweat as he thought of the inevitable outcome. He'd seen this sort of thing happen time and time again in the bars that he used to frequent in his haunted past. He stared at the table in front of him and clenched his fists as his pulse began to quicken. Anger began to boil deep inside him, one born of his hatred of men like these. It seemed that happiness was not meant for him. The demons that he'd buried inside were awakening against his will.

Steven scanned the gang, then squeezed his eyes shut. Seeing them reminded him of why he'd come here. He'd hoped to get away from their kind of trouble and never be tempted back into it again.

The inner struggles that Steven fought began when he was sent to Vietnam. There, innocence was torn from him as he developed the anger that would one day consume him—anger at the decisions made by foolish people that left his friends dying or worse. As those days went on, hope seemed to draw further and further away. After seeing countless deaths, Steven grew callous and accepted that he was meant to die like all the others for a cause he'd stopped believing in. He felt as though there was no hope for escape from the inevitable, and he went on, numb to life.

With no more hope, he'd learned a new way to deal with the overwhelming despair. He finally let the demons growing inside him kill the boy he'd been, which left only the angry, empty shell of a man. He no longer cared if he died. Often, he'd make reference to being a blade of dead grass in a field, whose only purpose was to be swept away by the flames.

All that remained in him was an anger and hatred that ended all his relationships. What was the use of trying to care for someone if they would only grieve when he died anyway? But death didn't come for Steven. His anger and hate turned to rage and kept him alive, day after day, as he killed those that would have killed him.

Upon realizing that his rage was his most deadly weapon, Steven learned a new way to live. As a weapon, Steven killed and brought pain to his enemies. In their suffering, he found a twisted sense of joy and purpose. On this sadistic path, Steven closed himself off from the rest of the world and allowed himself to be consumed by it.

Having no one left and nowhere to ease his suffering through pain and death, Steven reenlisted. His hollow feelings couldn't fit anywhere else but there. After a few years, the Special Forces recruited him for his almost supernatural ability to kill and survive. Through training and discipline, they gave him a forum for his skills and hidden, twisted desires. The Rangers and Special Forces didn't care what kind of disaster he would make of himself when sent back to the civilized world after the war. Vietnam needed to be won, and soldiers like Steven were needed to win it.

The few soldiers he would call friends during this time were all killed before coming home. His was a dangerous life, and he was the only one to survive the countless missions directed by his Special Forces unit. In time, his combat knife became the only thing of substance or importance. It was always with him as he continued to hunt and kill his enemies alone in the jungle.

But when there was no more war to fight, he came home for good, angrier and more dangerous than ever. Being home was more miserable than being in the war. No family, no friends, and no home. He'd pushed them all away, and many had passed on during the long years he'd spent fighting. He had no chance at redemption, should he have wanted it. No one was left to help with all his anger, and now there was no immediate outlet for his hate.

So Steven went looking for one. He found it among the rough and unwanted members of his own kind, those struggling with the aftermath of the war. Addiction to alcohol played no small part in his troubles. It drove him back to causing pain as a means of comforting his tormented mind. Steven remained strong, and his skills remained sharp long after the war. Most encounters ended in violence.

But this ruinous path could lead to only one end. Despairing and alone, he finally resolved that death was again the only path left to him. But try as he might, fight after countless fight, he couldn't find anyone up to the challenge of ending his miserable life.

It was during this time that Steven began to wake up in fits of drunken remorse every night. He kept having the same dream. His father would come to him with strong loving hands and pull Steven by the arm, away from the trouble that he so badly wanted to find. He would then remind him that who he'd become was not the person that was raised by his loving family and that he must change his ways.

So, Steven did the hardest thing he'd ever had to do. He began to seek a new path, away from the addictions. He resolved to honor his father and family

JN MASTER

in this struggle for a new life, no matter how hard the journey might prove.

But not enough time had passed between his painful past and the barroom in which he now sat. Unable to control himself and stay out of the trouble unfolding before him, Steven felt his demons delight in the chance to cause pain once more. Right or wrong, what he'd do to these men if they persisted with their troublesome agenda would not be understood by the kind townsfolk around him. He so wished to be part of this community, but the reality was plain. No matter where he went, he would never be able to outrun who he really was.

The leader of the bikers continued to lean on the bar and ignore the sheriff that stood between him and his men.

After gathering some courage, the bartender sat the glass he'd been cleaning on the large bar top and announced, "We're not gonna be serving you fellas. You know that."

The biker sneered. "Well, we can serve ourselves, 'cause this time we ain't leaving!"

The entire room sat hushed, eyes fixed on the sheriff. From their various positions around the room, the six other bikers turned their attention to their leader, ready to start the trouble they came to deliver.

Breaking the stillness in the room, two of the men moved toward the bar and their leader. As they did, they noticed Steven's table and rerouted toward it, recognizing that it presented the best chance of

80

trouble close at hand. It was also where the young girls were sitting.

Steven realized that he would have no choice of whether to get involved. This would be the end of the wonderful dream he'd developed over the last few days.

"You boys have caused enough trouble here," The sheriff stated with surprising tenacity for a man his age. "Now get the hell out!"

The burly gang leader laughed and turned around. "That's not happening. You were lucky we left last time. This time, you're all going to leave. Otherwise, you're going to need more townies!"

As the two men stared each other down, the four gang members at the pool table set their beer bottles on the felt top and began to push people toward the door. A few townsfolk rose in resistance. It was about to become a fight. It seemed that it would likely end in the bikers' favor this time. They were clearly there to get revenge.

The two men had nearly arrived at Steven's table. He continued staring blankly at the empty glass, rolling it between his thumb and forefinger. His foot tapped anxiously. The entire bar was locked in fear and seemed to be holding its breath in anticipation.

"Looks like we found our table, Kirk," one biker said to the other as they stared at Jill and the other girls. "You can stick around, sweetheart. Maybe we can take you for a ride later, since it didn't work out between us last time."

"We were just leaving, asshole!" Jill seethed. She gave Steven a desperate look, hoping for some sign of moral support. He continued thumbing his glass and staring blankly away from the men.

At the same time, the sheriff grabbed the leader of the gang by his shoulder in a vain effort to protect the people of the town. The drunken biker cursed and pushed back, hard. The sheriff tumbled into the table he'd been sitting at moments ago and fell to the floor.

Those at the table who were not knocked out of their chairs by the blow struggled to help the injured old man to his feet.

Upon seeing this cowardly first blow and the arrogant leader standing over the fallen sheriff, Steven couldn't restrain himself. He leaped to his feet almost involuntarily, knocking his chair to the floor. His hands shook with anger as he struggled to collect himself for the hell he was about to unleash. Jill and her friends slid quickly away in surprise. They hadn't anticipated this response.

Surprised by Steven's sudden reaction, the two bikers watched intently as they awaited Steven's next move.

Tuning his senses into the coming fight, Steven breathed deeply and focused on the odds that were stacked against him. The barroom seemed to be locked in time as he sized up all the bikers in the room. One by one, he took in their strengths and weaknesses and how he would engage them all in due time.

Having taken account of his new enemies, Steven reached down, lifted the pitcher from the center of the table, and drank it down to the last drop. The alcohol would make what he was about to do easier, as it had so many times before. The killer had awakened within him and couldn't be recalled. The beer tasted good on his lips again. With one last look at his injured friend across the room, he wiped his mouth on his sleeve and turned to fix his vengeance on the man nearest him.

"Well, who is this, sweetheart? Your brother?" The drunken biker sneered. "Like to keep it in the family out here, huh?" The other bikers laughed and began to move in Steven's direction. A few of the ranch hands started to rise from their chairs to block their way.

The men's chuckling faded into a deadly silence as the biker in front of Steven gave a deadly stare in return, recognizing that a brute like himself was about to challenge him.

Steven's glare shifted from the man in front of him to their leader, who was watching from across the barroom. A sinister smile curled Steven's lips, its message clear: he would soon be coming for him. The leader's sneer faltered.

"Look, boys! A Ranger pussy!" yelled the biker named Kirk, who had insulted Jill, as he pointed at the emblems on Steven's worn field jacket. "Probably a queer like the rest of those Army Rangers!" The biker lifted his shirt sleeve to reveal the marks of the Marine Corps on his shoulder. He expected the insult to drive Steven into throwing the first blow of the fight, and he awaited it now with a sadistic delight of his own in his eyes.

The leader, now starting to doubt the outcome of the situation, hollered over the crowd. "Everyone get the hell out of here, or some of you won't ever be leaving!"

Steven's rage boiled more furiously. He met Kirk's eyes and gave a taunting grin. "Not just a Ranger, you son of a bitch. And these people aren't going anywhere. This is their town, and it's you pieces of garbage that aren't going to be leaving now."

As soon as the threat left Steven's lips, Kirk erupted. Driven by drunken fury, he knocked one of Jill's friends out of the way as he charged forward with a raised fist. Without flinching, Steven grabbed Kirk's hand and drove it to one side to keep it from striking Jill. Kirk fell forward with the unexpected force of the deflected blow. He looked up at the rage that blazed back at him, and Steven drove the pitcher into his bewildered face.

Kirk crumpled to the floor amid the feet of scattering patrons and felt his bloodied and broken jaw.

"Son of a bitch!" Kirk mumbled through the blood filling his mouth. He spat on the floor and pulled himself up with the back of a nearby chair. He made another lunge for Steven. The townsfolk continued to race to get out of the way as Steven seized the big marine by the neck and drove him face-first into the heavy wooden table. As he held the struggling man, he looked up at his next target, now standing in disbelief of Kirk's failed attack.

Returning to his senses, this man continued his approach to help his defeated friend. As he did, Steven released Kirk, leaving the man gasping on the tabletop. Then, in one fluid motion, Steven turned and took him out of the fight permanently with a sharp rear kick that broke his leg at the knee. Kirk fell to the floor, screaming in agony. Steven flashed a gloating grin across the room to his friends. He knew that this would send the remaining gang members into a frenzy of anger and give him a better shot at controlling the outcome of the fight in their hysteria. To hear one of your own wailing in pain when your enemy stood between you was always demoralizing.

Steven's brutality seemed to have the desired effect as the man approaching him slowed, staring down at his friend. It appeared that he was no longer sure that his advance would be successful, as Kirk was a much better fighter than him. Finally, he stopped in his tracks. Sweat broke out on his brow as he looked at Steven's delighted expression.

The barroom seemed to be reeling in disbelief. Even the injured sheriff stared as he clung to the shoulders of the friends that held him up. It was plain to see that Steven had resolved to make each of the gang members feel the truth of his words—and he clearly had the capacity to do it.

Enraged, the four bikers across the room suddenly drove hard into the wall of cowboys blocking their path, and the room erupted in battling men. The hysteria that Steven had hoped to cause was now in effect.

Steven moved on the unsure man nearest to him. He now seemed like an idle threat on his path to destroy the leader of the gang. Steven clenched his fists tightly at his side as he drew nearer to the man. Dismayed and not wanting to face Steven alone, the man looked toward his other friends across the sea of tables. Realizing that help would not be coming, he turned back toward Steven and raised his shaking fists in defense. Blinking uncontrollably from the nervous sweat pouring into his eyes, the man held his breath in anticipation of the oncoming attack. He could feel the hatred blazing in Steven's eyes even as he looked away to steady his nerves.

The nearby table of friends, along with many of the townsfolk, took a chance to hurriedly exit the bar, overturning chairs in their haste. A few local ranchers and hands were now exchanging blows with the other gang members, empowered by Steven's besting of one of the more troublesome members of the gang. For the time being, these locals were giving back trouble of their own to most of the remaining bikers. They were tough, proud Wyoming men, all of them, but they had never fought anyone hell-bent on destruction and trained to kill like most of the bikers. But regardless of their fears, the locals who stayed weren't going to leave Steven's side.

With the intensity of the fight having risen around him, the leader of the gang took account of where his friends were. Trying to collect his cowardly wits while fixated on Kirk's screams of pain, the leader knew Steven would stop at nothing to destroy him. Thus, he snapped.

"You're all going to pay now!" He lunged at the still-shaky sheriff. He pounded his knurled fist into the shocked sheriff's face, despite the surrounding men's attempts to stop him.

Seeing this, Steven's rage was fanned to maddening fury. Now with desperate incentive to reach the leader, Steven grabbed a chair. The shaking biker before him was the only thing stopping him from getting to the leader harming the sheriff.

Though the quivering man was not much of a threat compared to some of the others that would soon arrive to fight him, Steven removed him from the fight anyway. He swung the heavy wooden chair and struck him with it. The chair broke across the side of the man's head and shattered his left arm. He immediately fell to the floor unconscious.

Stepping over his second neutralized enemy and a pool of blood, Steven moved quickly toward the leader. He knew that there would be little time to disable this man before his friend descended upon him, and Steven wanted to harm him most of all.

Calling on his combat experience, he calmed his breathing and gathered his thoughts. He felt that his chances of winning control of the engagement were good if he could neutralize the leader. A new sense of purpose rose within him, along with the wicked joy of being able to do what he was so good at. He would rid these fine people of this scourge once and for all. But he knew in doing so, with his addiction to violence, he would be powerless to stop it from going too far.

The leader of the bikers had begun fighting the men surrounding the sheriff. But before Steven was within reach of him, two of the other bikers burst from the battling crowd and descended upon him faster than he'd anticipated.

They grabbed Steven by the arms and throat and drove him backward, lifting him off his feet. Steven allowed it to happen as they pushed his back into the heavy wooden bar top. This worked in his favor, as it would give him cover on one side and a solid base to push back on. Suspended by their grasps, he rolled back to bring up his legs and wedge his feet solidly against their waists. As the men started to pound their revenge into his face, Steven kicked forward with considerable might, releasing himself from their grip and sending them tumbling backward into the brawl with their leader.

Disoriented, the two men quickly gathered themselves and leaped to their feet among the crowd they had toppled into. They were joined by a third biker that sprang free of the brawl. Grabbing a pool cue, he yelled, "We have a fighter here! Kill him!"

Steven was a brawler by nature, never very proficient at the martial arts that Special Forces had taught him. Rather than falling into a defensive posture, he stood with solid footing and straightened his field jacket in prideful defiance of their attack.

Following these men, some of the ranch hands came to the sheriff's aid and began trading hard blows with the leader of the gang.

The three men attacking Steven arrived within reach of him at the same time. The one with the pool cue swung it overhead and brought it down hard at Steven's face. Steven ducked out of the way, and it broke on the edge of the bar. He then punched the middle biker in the throat and sent him reeling backward. The other two men paused briefly at this sudden counterattack to focus on Steven as they collected themselves with whatever training their drunken minds could recall.

A moment later, the men lunged forward once more. The man still gripping the broken pool cue attempted to stab Steven with it, and the other man pulled a combat knife from under his old Marine Corps jacket. They both had murder in their eyes. Undaunted, Steven delighted at the deadly change in the game and responded in kind.

As the two men rushed him, Steven side-stepped out of reach and let them stumble into the bar top. Swiftly, he grabbed the pool cue and wrested it from the man's grip by breaking his thumb. As surprised as the man seemed, he showed no sign of being injured like Steven had expected and instead spun around to strike Steven with his injured fist.

The man got him on the right shoulder. The impact against his broken finger gave the drunken biker cause to roar in pain. As he did, Steven struck the man across the back of his head with the blunt end of the pool cue hard enough to knock him unconscious.

While he fell to the floor, his partner pushed the limp body to the side and smashed wildly into an unprepared Steven. Although he stumbled backward, caught in the man's grip, Steven quickly recovered his balance and set his feet against the wooden floor to stop the man in his tracks. He refused to fall at the hands of his enemy.

With his attempt thwarted, the enraged biker released him and instead grabbed the collar of his shirt. With his other hand, he swung his combat knife at Steven's stomach. Just before it could strike him, Steven seized the man's arm. The blade remained quivering in space just below Steven's stomach, suspended by both men's grips. Their strengths and wills battled against one another for control of the deadly blade.

As they stood in their struggle for life and death, the biker's strength began to falter. His anger turned to fear, and he looked up at Steven's face. Steven leaned toward his fearful face with a smirk.

"I told you none of you will be leaving."

Steven then began to push the knife back toward the biker's body. The man desperately tried to contend with Steven's strength, but it was no use. He knew he was going to die.

As he turned the man's blade back on him, the world around Steven began to grow dark. There was no difference between here and the kill-or-be-killed world of active war. He could feel himself growing stronger, as if he was slowly absorbing the other man's strength. He savored it, as it seemed to temper his rage. As he looked into the man's eyes, he could see they were those of a soldier, not so different from his own. But this man had made himself the enemy when he tried to take Steven's life, and now that enemy was going to die for it.

As the man continued to try and stop Steven from his deadly purpose, both were brought back to reality by the sound of a gunshot.

They looked up to see one of the nearby ranch hands lying on the floor amid the frenzy, holding a bloodied arm. In the unfolding chaos, two bikers raced out of the bar, with their cowardly leader following closely behind. The leader waved a gun at the men trying to stop him, some drawing guns of their own as they tried to stop his exit.

As the door swung closed behind the last fleeing biker, Steven looked at the bleeding young man in the crowd and then at the sheriff, who was also lying on the floor nearby. With a renewed rage burning inside him, Steven ended his struggle against the man in his grasp with a sharp jab of the blade.

As the man slumped against him, Steven pulled the knife from his bleeding chest and threw it down. The man dropped to the floor, gasping for help between bloody breaths. Steven stepped over him without a second thought and moved toward the door. His hands were sticky with blood, and he wiped them on his field jacket.

Focused only on catching the remaining three men before they could flee into the night, he passed by the group huddled around the sheriff. Looking up with caring eyes amid a broken face, the old lawman muttered faintly, "Let them go, son. It's going to be all right now."

Steven paused, snapping briefly from the rage, and looked down at the bloodied sheriff smiling back up at him. "Thank you for helping us." Grieved, Steven could say nothing in return.

Recognizing the face of a dying man, tears welled in Steven's eyes. He knew that these were the last words the sheriff would say to anyone, and he was saying them to him. He so desperately wanted to save him and these people, but there was nothing in the world Steven could do to save the sheriff now.

As the sheriff quietly stared up through his circle of friends, he closed his eyes and drew his last breath. How could all of this have happened? Why did the hell that always followed him have to come and ruin the lives of people that didn't deserve it? Had he not come at all, would this still have happened?

Tears began to stream down Steven's cheeks, and he heard the bartender yell from the kitchen behind the bar. "The state police are on the way with the ambulance!"

As the remaining patrons began to attend to the injured ranch hand, Steven heard a motorcycle fire up out front. He looked down at his blood-soaked hands, then cast his gaze back at the tavern door in fury.

Old Joe from the gas station rose and took one of Steven's bloodied hands in his own. Joe, who had remained by the sheriff's side throughout the ordeal and bore a few bloody cuts on his face, drew Steven's attention away from the door.

"You did what you could, son. Don't leave us this way."

Looking at the man, Steven could no longer see him through his tear-filled eyes. Beyond the door, he heard the second and third bikes firing up. Turning painfully away from Old Joe, Steven pulled his hand back and stared at the heavy wooden entrance, loathing the cowardly men about to escape on the other side. It was not enough for him to let it end like this. These men couldn't leave after what they had done.

Outside in the cold Wyoming night were the townsfolk who fled the oncoming fight. They were huddled on the far side of the parking lot, away from the danger of more gunshots and the confusion of the bikers fleeing the bar.

It was likely that the state police would take a long time to arrive from the distant town they were dispatched from. The townsfolk discussed what they might be able to do as they watched the three men warming up their motorcycles to flee.

Suddenly, the door of the bar flung open, spilling light onto the dirt of the parking lot. Moving with deadly purpose, Steven emerged gripping a pool stick in one hand and turned toward the men on bikes.

"Get down!" He shouted to the huddled townsfolk as he strode angrily toward the bikers.

He passed behind the line of trucks parked in the light of the bar's neon sign as the lead biker began to panic. Steven was the last man he wanted to face after seeing what he'd done to the more hardened members of his marauding group. The dim light illuminated the rage in Steven's face, and the biker now struggled to find the weapon he'd placed into the holster on his hip. Seeing this also, one of the other two men hurriedly put his bike into gear and began to spin his way through the gravel to escape.

Only one ranch truck stood between Steven's fury and the mounted men.

As he leaped up on the bed of the truck, the leader finally pulled his weapon free and fired wildly into the steel bed of the vehicle. The bullet glanced off the diamond plating and ricocheted into the night air, missing Steven by an inch.

Undaunted by the near hit and knowing that he now had the advantage, Steven leaped at the two men.

With a crash, he drove his shoulder into the leader. The momentum of the fall knocked the leader into the second man, and their bikes toppled. Both fleeing men were knocked to the ground and pinned under the running engines of their Harleys. The gun had flown from the leader's hand and slid underneath a nearby truck.

Quickly picking himself up off the ground, Steven walked over to the first of the two struggling men. He stomped on his flailing hand, crushing his fingers with a satisfying crack. Steven smiled as the man's screams of pain echoed through the still night air. He stepped farther into the neon glow, an unbroken pool cue in his hand.

Turning his attention to the third man still trying to escape on his motorcycle spinning in the gravel, Steven began his next assault.

The motorcycle finally gained traction in the dirt and gravel, but Steven suddenly emerged from the dust cloud it had created. He was illuminated in the haze by the red taillights like a demon emerging from hell. The biker looked back at Steven approaching, and panic contorted the biker's face.

Steven raced forward and shoved the pool cue through the spokes of the motorcycle's front tire, locking it just as the bike burst forward. The handlebars twisted from the man's grip, and the bike flipped forward on its side, throwing him into its headlights. Still heaving with rage and anger, Steven locked on to the terrorized man lying before him. As the biker began to collect himself from the dirt, he could see Steven's dark shadow of vengeance looming in the faint light.

Panicking and starting to mumble wildly to himself, the man stood up and limped across the highway, into the blackness of the night. Steven watched the man run for a moment, marking the direction in which he'd fled. He then reached down to retrieve half of the now-broken pool cue. Carefully examining it in his bloody hand, he tossed it back in favor of the sharper, more pointed half.

He turned his attention back to the other bikers, who were struggling to lift the idling motorcycles off their trapped bodies. They paused when they heard the heavy footsteps crunching slowly toward them. The steps fell silent amid the drone of their engines and spinning tires.

Steven's dark shape heaved as he breathed heavily, a blank look of murder in his eyes. The jagged object in Steven's hand glinted menacingly.

After what seemed like endless eerie minutes of Steven staring down the leader, the man with the broken hand began to plead for his life. Fixated only on the murderous leader, unmoved by the terrified man's words, Steven drove the sharpened end of the pool cue through his neck, silencing him forever.

In dismay, the leader began to whimper in fear. His upcoming death was plainly written on Steven's face. Urine dribbled onto the ground from over the man's boot and steamed on the hot exhaust pipe.

The townsfolk watched the scene unfold in horror. They couldn't see the trapped men behind the truck, but they could hear everything that was happening through the cold night air. Suddenly, Steven disappeared from their view, and they heard the unmistakable sound of wood breaking the leader's skull. Then there was absolute silence.

Steven reemerged. He began to walk up the dirt lot and into the darkness of the night on the far side of the highway, pursuing the man who had fled.

Still running as fast as his injured leg could carry him, the fleeing biker fell and cursed the sagebrush in his flight. After many minutes had passed, he stopped to catch his breath. The cold night air was now pungent with the smell of the broken sage leaves that covered him. Panting heavily and covered in sweat, he looked at the star-filled sky above.

The injured man figured he'd gone far enough to lose Steven. Everything had been silent back at the bar for some time now, and he decided that it was time to head back and devise some method of escape before the state police arrived. But as he turned and began to head in the direction of the distant lights, he saw a figure standing perfectly still just a few yards behind him. Panic rose in him as he recognized the man in the shadows.

Steven stood silhouetted against the light of the distant bar. Only the faint clamor of the bar patrons could be heard in the stillness as they took in the aftermath of the fight and what Steven had just done.

Too afraid to move, the man felt his heart sink as Steven finally broke the silence. "Your luck has run out."

Shaking with fear, the man raised his hands and began to plead. "Please! It wasn't my fight. It was that fat bastard back there on the Harley you knocked over. He's a piece of shit!"

"He *was* a piece of shit," Steven replied flatly.

The faintly heard conversation of the people in the parking lot went silent, as though they all were straining to hear the voices of the men far out in the prairie.

"Please, I won't come back here," the biker begged. "I'll never set foot in this town again! I have a daughter! Please!"

Steven walked through the sage until he was within arm's reach of the biker. The blood covering his coat and hands glimmered as he towered over the pleading man like an angel of death.

"You think that having a daughter matters to me?" Steven asked. "You're all the same, you rotten bastards! You killed a good man and have hurt these people for the last time."

"I didn't kill nobody!" The man glanced at the patch on Steven's shoulder. "I was in the army too!"

At that, Steven's hand caught the man by the throat and flung him onto the dusty ground.

Minutes later, Steven emerged from the darkness across the road from the bar. As he walked down the slope of the dirt lot, the townsfolk stood aside silently.

Steven didn't turn to face them as he walked toward the door. His anger hadn't subsided despite all the men being dead or too badly injured to fight anymore. It was as though he was in a trance. He'd fallen back into his old ways and could only see one answer now: kill the rest of the bikers inside so they could never return to this town and seek revenge.

Far off in the night, flashing lights were racing down the highway.

Steven looked up only at Jill, who shivered in her light coat. She was standing by her father, Bob, who must have raced to the bar upon hearing what had happened over the scanner. Jill leaned toward him and whispered something, prompting him to begin walking toward Steven.

"Don't go back in there son," Bob said. "These men aren't worth going to prison for the rest of your life. We all know what you did, and we're thankful for it. Old Joe heard the sheriff say it himself."

Steven turned his gaze to the ground and stood silent for a moment. The uncontrollable anger drained from his veins as Bob's words sunk in. He began to ponder what he'd just done and the consequences that were sure to follow. Bob's hand gently touched his shoulder.

Sirens hummed in the distance, along with the growing murmur of the townsfolk as they began to talk among themselves again. Feeling the intensity of the moment fade and Steven start to come to his senses, some of the people went back inside to help with fallen friends.

Finally looking up at Bob, Steven caught the man's thankful and understanding eyes. He could also see the sadness in the eyes of the people just beyond. Despite his expectations, they showed no fear of him, just sorrow for a man they wanted to help.

His hands shook. The blood had begun to dry, cementing broken pieces of sage leaves to his skin. He closed his eyes as the smell of the cold night air mixed with the sweet leaves. In that moment, he was reminded of the beautiful memories he'd made only a day before. He'd quickly grown to love these fine people. Before, he'd thought he had no love to give. He was thankful that Mr. Pearson hadn't been there to see what kind of monster he truly was. But just as quickly as he had these thoughts, he realized that his dream to live in this town was now lost.

Steven's hands fell onto his field jacket as he tried to wipe off some of the blood. Bob's hand remained on his shoulder, easing the pain he saw in the broken soldier.

As Steven tried to wipe the blood from his hands in vain, he knew that there would never be an end to the hell he was caught in. Any hope he had of escaping his demons was gone. Worst of all, this place would never be the same because of him.

He didn't notice the police cars until they were close enough to light the crowd. Breaking from his building sorrow, he turned to look out across the plains. The moon had just begun to rise, bathing the mountains in its pale glow. They were beautiful.

"Go, son," Bob said, patting him on the shoulder once more. "Go while you can. We'll take care of all this."

Steven didn't want to run anymore, but he didn't see another choice. With a last look at Bob's sincere face, he walked through the crowd toward the Bronco. Not knowing whether it was a good choice to leave, Steven pulled onto the highway and drove toward town. He didn't look back.

7

CHAPTER

A s the Bronco pulled away from the scene, the troopers sped past the bar and began to pursue Steven into the downtown area. Steven stared ahead, not noticing the patrol car until he was in front of the diner. His options were few. Adrenaline surged in his blood as he shifted into high gear and pressed down the gas pedal.

The single patrol car became three, all following with flashing lights and sirens blazing. Although he knew he couldn't outrun them, Steven pressed on anyway. He wanted nothing more than for all this trouble, and the horrible things he'd done, to have never happened.

But he couldn't be locked up in a cage for the rest of his life. The ghosts of the past now sat with him as the Bronco hit the main road just past the courthouse. He could hear the trooper's loudspeaker demanding that he pull over. Still, he kept going.

After many miles of chase, he passed Bob's general store. Finally snapping back from the numbness, he considered pulling over and ending it all right there on the shoulder of the road. What better place to die, especially compared to the many other places where his death had seemed inevitable? All he would have to do was get out and attack an officer without causing much harm. The police would surely put an end to his life for that. But the proud soldier in him purged that thought from his mind.

Steven drove for miles until the road began to turn slowly away from the mountains and broken country. Seeing his chance to act, he pulled sharply across the opposite lane and bounced through the dry swale running alongside the highway. The Bronco smashed through the barbed-wire fence that ran parallel to the highway.

In his rearview, Steven could see the patrol cars stop at the roadside, with no hope of giving chase across this rough country. They stepped out of their cars and into the headlights. He heard no shots and watched as they disappeared into the cloud of Wyoming dust he'd kicked up in his wake.

He continued to drive through the sage for a mile or so, dipping into small valleys and back up again. The Bronco climbed a hill, and Steven turned off his headlights as he went down the other side. Able to see as plain as day in the moonlight, Steven stopped the vehicle at the bottom of the hill, out of sight of the troopers. As he stepped out, the smell of the hot sage packed into the chassis of the Bronco hit him. He collected his thoughts about what to do next.

Leaving the vehicle idling, he walked to the top of the hill and looked back at what the state police were doing. They were bathed in headlights, but he strained to see if any had decided to follow his tracks and continue the chase across the rough prairie. None had dared yet, but he knew he would have little time before they decided to.

His path was clear now. He must keep going. There would be nothing left but prison for having killed those men. He would not spend the rest of his life trapped in a cell with his unresolved misery.

Steven would hole up in the mountains and try to pull his shattered life back together again. Someday he might try to come back to the world, but for now, he could survive just as well in the wilderness, as he had so many times during the war. His peace lay ahead of him, and he would find it again. Maybe in the footsteps of his youth, like where he'd found it just days before. The mountains were calling to him.

He returned to the Bronco, needing to put as many miles of rough country behind him as possible. He began to pick his way across the plain in the dark hours ahead. As he did, the passing time allowed him to think over what he'd done.

He hated that the monster inside him was still capable of doing such things. But at the same time, he was glad that his madness, in some way, had helped those people. Some even seemed grateful for it, like

Bob. He wished the night could have ended differently, that he could have saved the sheriff or that the trouble had been avoided. He wondered if he could ever be anything other than a trained killer. Yet, for the first time in his life, it seemed to have a bigger purpose that he couldn't explain. It was plain that the situation at the bar would have ended worse for those good people if he hadn't been there, and the wickedness of those dangerous men would have continued to haunt them. Now, those enemies were gone.

Coming back to his task at hand, Steven knew the Bronco would be easy to track. He remembered Mr. Pearson's story about the broken lands that lay somewhere near the base of the mountains. If he could get far into that country and then continue on foot, he would be impossible to find. He was a master of evading detection in places like those mountains, and once there, his fate would again be his own.

Picking his way through the valley bottoms and sagebrush, he covered dozens of miles over the remaining hours of the night. No cattle or living creature could be seen in the moonlit landscape, save for a surprised coyote that raced out from in front of him.

He eventually left the smoother terrain and entered rough, rocky ground that spilled from the mouths of the valleys on either side of him.

The first time he stopped was to check that the 4x4 had clearance to cross a deeper dry wash. Steven could hear the nearby buzz of a rattlesnake as he stepped from the cab. He'd dealt with many cobras in Vietnam, so he was unafraid.

The dried blood on his hands had collected dust and made gripping the steering wheel difficult as he pressed on into the night once more. The cold had set in, and it kept him alert. His progress slowed as he drove deeper and deeper into rough terrain. Finally, he could go no further without rolling his vehicle into a deep draw that he carefully negotiated the four by four alongside. It was time to go on foot.

Steven backed the Bronco to the head of the draw. He then continued to steer in reverse through the narrow, winding ravine until he was blocked by some boulders. Here, he would conceal the vehicle. He knew that when it was eventually discovered, it might fool his pursuers into thinking he intended to return to the road at some point and was hiding close by. He had no such intention, however, and now hoped that abandoning his trusty Bronco might buy him precious time to escape.

After turning off the engine, Steven gathered as much gear as he could for the journey ahead. He left his sleeping bag and the clothes he couldn't wear in the back of the vehicle—a further attempt to fool his pursuers into believing that his intention was to return to the Bronco. As a final decoy, he left the keys still hanging in the ignition.

He taped his knife to a shoulder strap of the ruck-sack he'd traveled with since the war, then tried to wash the blood from his hands with the little bit of water he had left in the canteen. When he finished, Steven began his climb through the sage and rocks toward freedom.

At the top, he paused to catch his breath, staggered by the silence of the magnificent moonlit wilderness. He once more collected his thoughts and set his course into the broken country ahead.

He moved silently under the silken blue sky, feeling the cold of midnight drawing into his coat. Slowly ascending to the top of the higher ridge, he heard only the sound of his boots crumbling the small rocks beneath. On the far horizon, he could see the shimmering lights of the small town and the ranches scattered throughout the countryside. No sign of pursuit. Turning away from what could have been, he looked to the rising mountains across the badlands and the uncertain life ahead.

He was a man wary of everything being taken from him, be it by his own doing or others'. Now it seemed there were enemies to be found at every turn, so he would go where there were no more to be found. He'd been driven by his own hands into a life of exile before, and now his destiny had been laid bare and unwritten once more.

He was comforted by the silence around him. The purity of the loneliness, despite everything that had happened, was now a welcome friend returning from the past. Out here in the vastness, he couldn't hurt anyone anymore.

He pressed on through the night, rising and falling into deeper and deeper terrain, until the moon finally dipped below the horizon and the first glow of a cold dawn started to chase away the countless stars left in the moon's wake.

Steven paused occasionally to look ahead on his path. The mountains seemed no closer than they had been from the road, but now the town could no longer be seen over the horizon. Feeling the cold finally biting to his core, he vowed to travel until the first rays of sunlight struck him, as it would be too cold to sleep without a fire until then.

Soon, the glow of the red predawn horizon began, and the first birds of morning could be heard stirring in the valley he now traveled through. No sign of cattle or fence line could be seen in any direction, which assured him that he was on a path that led far from people. This had to be the country that Mr. Pearson had described.

Finally, feeling the first rays of the dawn strike the back of his neck, Steven knelt against the side of a large boulder, just below the rim of the valley, and removed his pack. He carefully cleared a small patch of sandy soil behind a nearby sage bush to rest for a few hours. The position also offered concealment and a view of his back trail—useful in the unlikely event that he was being hunted. Lying down, he soon fell fast asleep in the warm morning sun.

He awoke after what must have been only a few hours of rest, as he noted from the high angle of the now-hot sun. Steven stood up cautiously into the bright daylight and looked around. He marveled at the endless beauty of the red and orange valley walls around him. Small, gnarled juniper trees grew here and there amid a sea of greasewood bushes and scattered yucca plants. Perfect cover to avoid being seen.

Steven ate some of the trail mix that he'd saved from his trip into the mountains some days before. Feeling a little better after his rest and meager meal, he set off in a direction opposite of what he'd been traveling the previous night.

Pulling his pack back onto his broad shoulders, Steven paused one last time to check his back trail. Satisfied that no one was within sight, he continued on his way.

He crested over the valley wall and began to move up and over the broken terrain. Stopping occasionally for a drink from his canteen, he used the breaks to correct his bearing toward the endless rocky canyons ahead. After a short time, he made his way to the top of another high ridge. From that vantage point, Steven spied a large valley that promised an easier walk to the mountain's base.

After a few more hours of bushwhacking toward the valley, through the ever-increasing sage and greasewood, Steven turned down a juniper-choked dry bottom that led into the side of the larger valley.

Now certain that he had a solid head start on any-one looking for him, Steven tucked into the shade of the junipers framing the end of the small box canyon and marking his entrance into the valley.

Throwing himself down for another nap until sunset could provide some cooler air in which to travel, Steven breathed deep, exhausted breaths. His water was almost gone, and he needed to conserve as much of it as he could. Lying on the hard sandy ground, he fell fast asleep.

He awoke from his fitful rest with a start. Sitting up quickly, Steven was cold from lying on the ground well into the evening. Apparently, he was more tired than he'd thought.

Gathering himself and scratching some bug bites, Steven realized that he must have slept right past the sunset and into another cold night. Taking in his surroundings in the deadened silence of the evening, he stood and resumed his trek into the moonlit valley floor.

Crossing onto the opposite side of the dry valley, Steven sipped the last drops from his canteen and shoved it back into his army web belt. He adjusted his pack so it would not cut into his shoulder as he stepped onto a game trail and made his way through the darkness.

The hardened dirt trail must have been worn into the ground by game traveling along this route over the ages. It now provided the less-strenuous walking that he'd hoped for and left no sign of his footfalls as he trod along. Having grown weary with the chase, this easier passage lifted his spirits and allowed him to focus on the task of surviving in this wilderness. The greatest concern he had at the moment was finding some clean water.

With the chilling effect of dehydration setting in, Steven pressed on and up the valley floor. He looked like a ghostly figure drifting through the shadows of the starry night. Dawn began to brighten the eastern skyline.

When he realized that he could go no farther before the heat of the day came, he found a suitable place to make his bed for another few hours of sleep. As the sun rose once more, he was pleased to have the sunlight chasing the cold from his bones as he again rose from the dirt.

It was time to start looking after his need for water, then find a shelter in which he could rest more soundly. The food in his pack would carry him until he could hunt or trap a few of the area's plentiful rabbits. Risking a fire might soon be possible as well.

Looking ahead, Steven noticed that the mountains were much closer than before. They began to fall away into the broken land on their western shoulder. The tapering seemed to offer a wide passage into the high plains. The pass would not be noticeable from below or in town. It was the perfect place to hole up until he could figure out what to do next.

Moving on, Steven passed the heads of small box canyons that dropped into the larger valley along the game trail. Still no sign of cattle or humans. Birds called to one another from the walls within the small canyons, echoing in the morning stillness. His breath puffed out in front of him as he strode along the trail in the cool fall morning, and he marveled at the golden-orange beauty of this place in the sunlight.

The air was thick with the smell of sage and the citrus scent of juniper needles heating in the sun. Before long, his breath was no longer visible, and by noon his thirst could no longer be ignored.

As the sun passed high overhead, Steven stepped across a small, dry creek bed at the mouth of one of the steep-walled canyons to his right. Pausing in the loose gravel, he noticed some small rocks that had been recently turned by the intermittent passing of flowing water. Hoping to find this water farther up, he decided to break from his current path and follow the dry creek into the canyon.

As he made his way along his new path, Steven passed through small stands of yellowing aspen trees, further heightening his hopes of some water ahead. The warm afternoon air flowed lazily past, carrying the incense-like scent of the aspens.

Steven felt eased in his passage along the winding course of the dry stream. The wall of the canyon began to rise sharply above him. As he rounded the bend in the valley floor, the sun suddenly disappeared behind a shoulder of the heights above, leaving him in cool shadows.

After a short climb along this course, Steven came upon what he desperately sought. Glimmering in sunlight ahead lay a pool of crystal-clear water beneath the rooted bank of some nearby aspen trees. Steven knelt at its edge and removed his pack. He drew in a long, cool drink. His thirst was such that he didn't care if he purified it first. The water felt cool and smelled clean enough. The dust in his mouth washed away along with his weariness with each mouthful he drank.

As he leaned back into the gravelly bed of the stream and wiped his lips, his thoughts drifted back to his father and uncle. They'd drunk from a pool like this when he was young. He shifted to a sitting position against his resting pack and began to take in the rays of the sun through the silent forest. As evening drew near, the pleasant memories began to chase away the darkness of his recent deeds.

After several minutes adrift in thought, Steven began to consider a place to shelter for the coming night. He surveyed the landscape around him and noted a small notch in the canyon wall to his left. The sun wasn't far from setting behind the high rim of the canyon.

Steven filled his canteen and washed his hands and face thoroughly of dirt and dried blood. Then he shouldered his pack once more and made his way through the small forest toward the outcrop.

Considering his desire to feel the first light to warm him in the coming morning, Steven risked not having the cover of the shadows. As he climbed the base of the slope leading to the ledge, he was pleased that the view from his chosen side of the canyon would afford him a better view back down the valley floor. From here he would be able to spot anyone that may have tracked him this far and escape quickly.

After ascending from the canyon floor covered by the first fallen leaves of the year, Steven picked his way up the scree-covered slope to where it met the steep wall of the box canyon. A cottontail rabbit burst from underfoot as he made the short climb toward his hide. The rabbit gave him hope, as he would surely find others when it came time to replenish his provisions.

Steven pulled himself onto the ledge and crawled into the opening of the alcove to find a level under-cut with a dry floor free of debris and pack rat nests. Turning to look at the forest below, he noted that it also offered the concealment he'd hoped for.

He walked to the back of the small shelter, re-moved his pack, and leaned it against the rear wall. Sitting on a boulder overlooking the pool of water below and the opposite side of the box canyon, Steven pondered all that had happened once more.

The last birds of the day flew by on the way to their evening perches. Their movement brought him back from the internal darkness that he'd begun to fall into. The setting sun painted the canyon in majes-tic hues of red amid the scattered greens of the small pines that clung to its base.

Still locked in a daydream, Steven breathed in the warm notes of the rising valley air as the final rays of light leaped over the top of canyon walls. Longingly watching the light fade, he felt as though it was his only friend after his exodus from the plains and town below. With nothing more to do, and weariness set-ting in, Steven made as good a bed as he could from the few dry clothes he'd kept bundled in this pack.

He bit off a few chunks of jerky and took a long drink from his canteen to get him through the night. Lying in his makeshift bed, he turned his face toward the rock and drifted to sleep. The first stars of the evening began to appear in the velvety night sky as he dozed.

The night brought with it the dead silence that only the most remote places know. The dim lights of an incoming thunderstorm began to flash against the canyon walls as it made its way across the mountains high above him. Even the rumblings of thunder were too far off to be heard.

Steven's dreams walked him through the mountains above. Joined by his father and uncle, they passed through the sun-bathed woods in pursuit of a majestic bull elk.

They laughed from their perch high on the rocks, not caring about spooking it but rather delighting in telling tales to the boy sitting among them. The men talked of Steven's grandfather and how much he loved being outdoors when they were young. He'd taught them how to hunt and fish and survive in the wilds of the Pennsylvanian forests and fields. Steven happily swung his feet as they talked about how much they wished he could have been with them in the beautiful Wyoming country.

As his dream went on, Steven slowly felt himself growing into a man on those rocks. The men beside him drifted into a mist of memory, and he soon found himself sitting alone as the man he now knew himself to be. The sunshine he'd been bathing in slowly drifted under the rim of the far peaks, and night began to settle around him. Once again finding himself alone, the hollowness that seemed to define him revealed itself in his heart once more. Mourning the passing of his innocence, Steven sat staring into the staggering beauty of the slowly darkening valley below him. The last wisps of warm scented pine air drifted up from the forest below to the rocky outcrop on which he was seated.

Feeling peace and calm in the vastness, Steven's attention was suddenly drawn to the shadows of the forest below. At first, he was not certain whether what he heard in the trees was a trick of his mind or just the falling of cold waters in the still starry night. But as he listened more carefully, he was certain that he heard the soft voice of a young woman rising above the dark pines.

Against his will, the dreaming Steven rose to his feet and began to descend through the rocky heights. It was as though she was calling to him through song. Her voice wrote desire into his heart, and he couldn't dissuade himself. He had to find the young woman.

As he descended the mountainside toward the voice in the pines, he heard his father call after him.

"Steven! Don't go that way, son. Know that we will always love you."

Startled, he turned to see his father and uncle standing on the rocks that he'd just been sitting upon. They faded into memory again, disappearing forever into the night sky.

Steven felt utterly alone as they left, but still he heard the song from the dark forest. The song drew away from him, and the veil of stars above became covered by approaching storm clouds. A sharp wind struck him as it began to roar through the rocks and crevices. It blew dust into his eyes and choked him. Feeling as though he was being driven from the heights, Steven turned to follow the beckoning voice of the young woman in the valley.

Steven finally entered the shelter of the valley below the raging winds and clouds above. Passing from the open slope into the edge of the lodgepole pines, he stepped onto a soft blanket of needles that covered the ground along the edge of the thick forest. As he walked deeper into the dark wood, the sound of the raging storm above seemed to fade into silence. The needles beneath his feet grew thicker, muffling all sound save that of his own deep breath. The voice could no longer be heard in the stillness.

As Steven quietly pressed forward among the silent trunks, the calmness of the valley eased his troubled mind, and his senses were filled with the scent of warm pines once more. He felt as though he walked on an island protected from the turbulent seas of life. Then his thoughts turned to finding the source of the voice. Straining his gaze into the darkness, Steven caught faint movement ahead of him.

Although he caught only glimpses, he could see that it was a young woman dressed in white, passing gracefully between the rough trunks of the trees. He began following her through the silent wood as she continued down the valley away from him.

She turned to face him from a distance and began to sing her intoxicating song once more. Steven's heart once again swelled with desire. He moved faster now, breaking the sharpened branches that stood between him and the beautiful young woman.

Her song led him further down the valley, though she never turned to face him again. Steven did his best to catch up to her. As he raced ever faster after her, sharp pine branches tore at his clothing and skin despite his efforts to weave in between the darkened forest's tree trunks. He could smell the pungent black soil beneath the bed of needles being kicked up by the heavy footfalls of his boots. It felt as though the woman would be his destiny, a path away from all his darkness and despair, if he could only be by her side.

He raced forward in the dark wood, afraid he wouldn't be able to reach her. Looking up through the tops of trees that surrounded him, he could see the storm clouds racing across the mountaintops at unbelievable speeds. It was as if time were moving around him at an incredible pace. He pushed himself ahead in desperation, but still he couldn't get any closer to the young woman.

Suddenly, the dark mountain pine turned into a thick jungle of darkened green. Steven paused in shock. He swept his hands across heavy, wet leaves. He'd seen leaves just like these during the war. As he adjusted to his surroundings, the woman's voice carried over the sounds of rain falling through the dark canopy and splashing heavily on leaves about him.

Remembering fighting in this same forest, Steven moved slowly through the rainforest, following the sound of the young woman's voice. Suddenly, he began to hear the enemy calling in the darkness around him. Half believing that they were there, half suspecting that none of this could be real, he maintained a cautious pace toward the still-singing voice. He began to catch fleeting glimpses of the woman through the dense jungle.

Despite the foreign enemy voices around him, the only fear he felt was of losing sight of the woman again. This fear began to turn into anger as the enemy voices recalled memories that he'd tried to forget.

The wet jungle leaves soaked his clothes, and his drenched hair hung over his brow. He swept it back from his eyes, and his hands left a warm, dark liquid on his face. They were covered in blood. He didn't know where it had come from, but the feeling of it on his hands again gave him unimaginable strength. A strength that seemed to leave him with no fear or apprehension.

The enemy voices stopped abruptly, as did the voice of the young woman. Steven looked around to see where they had gone so suddenly, then continued pushing his way through the thick, wet undergrowth toward where he'd last heard the song. Soon amid the dense forest and dark rain falling loudly through the treetops, he spotted a clearing.

Now that he couldn't hear the woman's song, Steven knew she awaited him in the opening ahead.

He found himself stepping into a dry, open field—a stark contrast to the wet, miserable jungle now just feet behind him. Lush sweetgrass lay at his feet. The field stretched from the edge of the jungle to the horizon, where it met the star-filled heavens above. He stood silently in the calm of early morning twilight. The stars sparkled blue, white, pink, and red against the soft velvet sky. This dreamlike place made Steven feel warm and comforted once more.

To his great delight, his eyes fell upon that which he'd sought. Amid the sea of grass stood a beautiful woman robed in a soft, white cotton dress. He couldn't see her face clearly, but she was reaching toward him.

Though his heart burned with desire, he paused. He just stood there, looking at her from across the field. Watching her beckon him silently forward, he suddenly felt as though this was the last morning of his life. If he went forward, he would join the beautiful woman and forever walk with her into the eternal morning rising behind her.

Entranced by her radiance, he once more heard the voices of the enemy in the jungle. They called for him in the darkness beyond, as did the voices of friends he'd lost in the war. They didn't cry for help but seemed to be calling him back to the hell from which he'd just emerged—a hell that Steven wished to leave far behind. Their voices broke him from his blissful moment. He felt the guilt that he'd long tried to repress come pouring from deep inside his chest. He struggled to keep it from consuming him, but it turned into rage, as it had done so many times before. He hated himself for his weakness.

As his mood changed, the woman began to walk toward him across the pleasant starlit grasses. She started singing again. Her song had turned into a lullaby, soothing Steven's torn heart and flaring his desire to join her in eternal peace. He couldn't take his eyes off her. She whispered to him in song, hand extended, beckoning him to her. He desperately wanted to step forward and take it, but he stood against his will on the edge of the wood, seized by his anger.

Her lullaby reached a crescendo. The crying voices of the enemy faded, and those of his lost friends became indistinguishable from murmuring voices he didn't recognize. Both his friends and the strangers seemed desperate to stop Steven from crossing the field. They seemed to draw closer to him in the jungle just beyond.

His heart conflicted, Steven turned away from the approaching woman to look for those who would stop him. The star-filled sky above suddenly fell dark with storm clouds, and a young man stepped out from the deep shadows of the wood.

Steven didn't recognize him. The young man was dressed in the weather-worn clothing of a cowboy. He walked quickly toward Steven, holding a small golden cross in his right hand. He cast a fearful, angry look at the young woman.

"You must come back!" the young man said, meeting Steven's eyes. He raised his crucifix like a beacon for him to follow. "Now!"

The lullaby that still drifted softly across the field now brought with it an icy cold breeze. As the chill cut at Steven, a flash of lightning erupted from the gathered clouds and struck deep in the jungle. Steven didn't turn his gaze from the young man. The young woman was no longer there, and he felt a sudden pain in his head, as though he were waking from a head injury.

Heavy rain began to fall from the clouds overhead. The young woman's lullaby had stopped entirely, and the young man faded into mist. The world grew silent as the cold rain fell heavily on his shoulders.

Steven turned to look for the beauty that he knew was no longer there. In one last moment of weakness, he'd hoped she would still be standing there, waiting to lead him from the troubled paths he'd grown so weary of traveling.

But instead of the beautiful young woman, what stood before him was unimaginable. A massive, dark figure stood in her place. From a distance, it appeared to be robed in black and much larger than the tallest of men. Darkness radiated like smog from its sleeves, over large, elongated hands. It clenched its clawed fingers, whose bony cracking could be heard all the way across the field. But Steven's eyes were drawn most deeply to the creature's face hidden beneath the darkened hood. There blazed two sinister snake eyes of bright yellow, clearly visible from afar amid the black vapor pouring from beneath the tattered cloak.

The creature glared at Steven with malice he could feel in his bones. The coming sunrise slowly brightened the field, and it finally broke its stare and lifted a cloth from the ground at its feet. The white dress of the beautiful young woman was soaked in blood.

Upon seeing this, Steven didn't feel terror. Instead, rage built up from deep inside. It had taken the young woman that would have been his savior from this wretched life. The spell he'd fallen under evacuated his mind, and Steven yelled in defiant rage at the beast. He stepped forward with a lust for revenge, a fire of his own in his eyes. The beast staggered backward at Steven's advance and screeched in the voice of the young woman. "No!"

A violent clap of thunder rumbled far beyond the canyon walls, waking Steven from his dream. He was covered in cold sweat. The stars that had hung so brightly above the rim of the canyon were now veiled by the clouds of an approaching storm. Steven felt the gentle vibration of the distant thunderclap against his cheek, which was still pressed to the dry alcove wall.

Disoriented by his dream, Steven slowly became aware of the flashes of light illuminating the shelter about him. Rubbing the dust and cold sweat from his eyes, he remembered where he was and rolled to face the opening.

Cautiously, he crawled over the boulder near the entrance, feeling as though someone was nearby. Holding his breath in anticipation, he listened for voices and looked for lights among the trees below.

As he scanned the darkness, he was stricken with the realization of a mistake he'd made earlier. He'd foolishly forgotten to disperse his tracks in the moistened sand by the pool. Fear grew in his chest, and he couldn't fight the sense that he was being watched by someone or something unseen in the darkness. This gut instinct had served him well in the war. It was like a miserable supernatural gift, along with all the other terrible skills that still haunted him.

After many long minutes, his anxiousness departed with a strike of lightning that was close enough to be seen and heard. Steven turned back to his sandy bed along the rock wall, thankful for the false alarm and the shelter he'd carefully chosen to save him from the incoming rains falling farther up the valley.

He crawled back to his makeshift bed and watched as the storm sent sheets of lightning over the box canyon. Softly, rain began to drip over the lip of the overhanging rock, accompanied by a warm breeze that blew the droplets into the shelter at his feet. Soon after, the rain began to pour more fluidly over the face of the shelter as the storm began to lick the rim of the canyon.

Steven gazed into the dark rain and felt so very alone. Finally, he lay down on his dry bed and chased away the eroding thoughts of his sorrow once more.

Taking one more deep breath of warm humid air, he looked over his shoulder before committing to sleep. A foul scent drifted on the breeze. He turned on one shoulder and rolled to stare into the darkness beyond the opening. The smell passed as suddenly as it came. With drooping eyelids, he drifted once more to an uneasy rest as the storm continued to rage.

He awoke the next day to a clear and damp morning. He rose slowly, having not rested well after catching the smell. He'd woken up more often than he'd hoped in order to scan his surroundings. No sign of an intruding beast could be found on the bone-dry floor of the alcove.

As Steven collected himself, he was thankful for the heavy rains that had surely washed away all signs of his passing in the lands below, including the thoughtless set of tracks he'd left at the pool. He would be untraceable by man or hound, as the storm had raged far out in the direction that he'd fled from.

Feeling assured that his freedom was absolute and that he could loiter as long as he needed, he waited in the alcove for the sun to rise. He wanted to make certain that the soil would be dry enough to try to establish a more permanent camp somewhere nearby without leaving deep tracks.

Eating a small breakfast of jerky and trail mix, Steven watched the world wake in the canyon before him. The golden leaves of the aspen grove caught the morning sun as they dried, and a gentle fog rose toward the rim above. Another warm day was at hand, and soon he would move farther up the small box canyon. All thoughts of the strange scent left his mind in the peaceful morning, and he began to debate the potential outcomes of the choices to be made. He finally resolved that he would wait out the winter somewhere between there and the mountains. Going back to the world would be out of the question for a very long time, and he was more than capable of surviving indefinitely in the wild.

His mind drifted to his deeds leading to this moment. He didn't have remorse for them, although he struggled not to hate himself for being naive enough to believe he could outrun his past. And for dragging those poor people into his madness.

After struggling not to fall back into the anger that always followed thoughts like these, Steven stood and took a cautious look down the valley. Coming back to the tasks at hand, certain that he was in the clear and that the ground was sufficiently dry, Steven collected his belongings and slung his pack over his shoulders.

Stepping down onto the dried boulders, he looked up into the box canyon ahead. He could see quite a ways away. The canyon walls steepened, and the valley bent many times as it marched further up the broken country. It narrowed in some places and opened again into stands of more golden aspen. It was beautiful to see.

As Steven stepped down to the next boulder, his eyes caught something out of place to his left. A large set of footprints descended the slope from below the alcove he'd been sheltering in. Assuming they must have been left by the animal he'd smelled the night before, Steven moved across the slope to examine them.

His heart leaped from his chest. The tracks were unmistakably made by large human feet.

8

CHAPTER

Now on full alert, Steven followed the tracks back to the valley floor, where they disappeared into the thick foliage.

He paused in the cover of the forest and cautiously scanned the area. He barely dared to breathe for fear of seeing someone. This person clearly knew he was there and would likely not be far away.

Anger swelled inside him, and he reached to adjust his knife, should he have need of it. Set on not being taken by surprise, Steven embraced his instinct to hunt for the intruder. He needed to know who they were and what their intentions might be.

As he moved through the aspen wood, he worked his way back to the creek bed, which was now full from the night's rain. It babbled loudly as it fell from the mountain above. The sound would help mask his movement during his search.

His mind was uneasy. What would he do if he caught up to whoever left the tracks? Surely they had to know he was there. Otherwise, why would they have approached his position so cautiously in the dead of night? And were they the cause of the strange smell?

Could it have been a rancher that had watched him take shelter from a distance? Could it have been someone searching for him? Why had they not made their move when they exposed themselves on that slope?

No tracker would have let themselves be so easily discovered by scent or track. Steven himself didn't smell that bad, even after his sweaty escape over the last few days. It certainly could not be a hunter of his caliber. In the war, he would mask his scent by covering himself in mud or washing his garments as frequently as time allowed. A good hunter would not have made such a mistake.

Regardless of who it was, Steven needed to know why they were there and make sure not to allow them an upper hand or give away his whereabouts.

Cautiously, he moved through the timber, searching for more signs.

By the time the sun passed into midday, Steven hadn't encountered a single trace of the intruder. With his questions spurring him forward, he continued up the valley floor along the stream. He finally stopped just before dark to refill his canteen in the quickly drying stream.

Having covered a few miles during his search, Steven found himself much farther up the canyon.

Here the steep rocky walls drew closer together. Steven decided that this would be a good place to make another meager camp for the night and possibly catch anyone else in the canyon by surprise, should they come back.

Recalling countless nights being hunted in the bush in Vietnam, he chose a position near the narrowest point of the canyon. There was good cover to lay up for the night a little distance from the now-quiet stream. In this location, Steven could only be approached on one side, and he had a good view across the canyon and a sheer wall to his back.

While waiting for darkness to fall, he began the work on his tiny shelter, prioritizing camouflage over comfort. He gathered a few dead branches into a small pile against a sandy boulder at the base of the cliff. Occasionally, he'd stop to look and listen for signs of the mystery person out in the fading light.

With his shelter complete, Steven removed his pack and slipped silently under the loose cover. He pulled the old rucksack into the entrance for additional camouflage and a makeshift pillow. The night promised to be warm again, and he hoped that there would be no more storms coming down out of the mountain to drench his hidden bed.

As in the war, his intention was to detect anyone approaching or passing by and have the advantage of observing what they were up to. Vigilant, he remained there in his earthen bed, which smelled of the fall leaves and the sandy soil beneath him. The warm air of the night was still and didn't begin to cool too quickly, as he'd hoped. The bed underneath him felt rough and its coolness began to seep into his clothing as the night wore on.

Every half hour, he would peer over his pack into the shadowed forest in front of him. As morning drew near, the sky became darker than anything he'd seen, despite the gleaming dots of stars. No sign of an approaching storm. Just utter darkness and silence.

Feeling that he could rest a little more peacefully with dawn soon approaching, he attempted to take longer naps between watches. The twilight of morning couldn't be far off now.

He woke with a start into pitch blackness and fought to remember where he was. After a few minutes of gathering his bearings, he became aware of an icy cold that now surrounded him in his uncomfortable bed. Looking up, he saw just the cobalt sky between the rims of the tall canyon walls. There were fewer stars than before.

Still, he dared not move, he was struck by a feeling that he was no longer alone. The haunting cold felt unnatural, as though it were coming from the very darkness in front of his shelter. That's when he smelled the foul odor once more.

Now alert, Steven quietly unfastened the button holding his large knife to his pack strap. It had been with him on all his combat tours and used to deadly effect dozens of times. He no longer carried a gun, for the knife had never failed to keep him alive or dispatch his enemies. A silent companion that never judged him, the knife was always there when he needed it.

He shut his eyes tightly, hoping his fears were unfounded. Steven drew one more breath of icy, foul air before daring to look into the woods ahead of him. The odor was growing stronger and reeked of death.

Straining against the darkness, he listened one more time before cautiously lifting his head above the pack. With eyes peering just over its top, Steven began to adjust to the darkness in front of him. Nothing moved as the valley shadows came into view. He searched for the source of the smell, but he was looking too far ahead.

As he shifted to focus on the surroundings closer to him, his gaze locked on to an out-of-place shadow. He hadn't noticed it before, but now it drew his full attention. The chill of the icy air struck his spine. There was something there in the darkness.

He stared for what seemed like an eternity. His hand gripped his knife tightly. Whatever it was, it appeared to be standing in the path he'd taken to make his bed. He couldn't tell what it was—it seemed like an amorphous black mass—it seemed to be staring back at him.

The darkness around it seemed to grow and deepen, almost as if it weren't there at all, as if it were only a trick of his tired eyes. But the smell still emanated from the creature mere yards in front of him. Any thought that it was just an illusion of the night immediately left his mind when it slowly lowered onto the forest floor.

His heart raced, not in fear but rage. He knew an encounter was inevitable. The massive black shape skulked silently toward him upon the dark forest floor. Steven prepared to spring at whatever it was, waiting for it to burst upon his hide. He remained perfectly still as it drew nearer. It had to know he was there. The choice to fight or flee was now upon him.

But the shadow stopped just shy of the pack at the opening of his hide—so close he could hear its faint, ragged breath driving the pungent odor at him. Then he heard the unimaginable.

"I see you, child," it hissed, softly, with a voice more bestial than a human.

Without further thought, Steven lunged and struck it with his pack, his other hand clutching the knife. The shadow screeched in anger. Close enough to deliver a deadly blow, Steven slashed his blade across its blackened head.

Roaring again in terror, the beast struck Steven with an arm, hurling him into the timber below. He smashed through a few low branches before hitting the ground hard and rolling back onto his knees. He still clung to his knife.

The beast, or whatever it was, bellowed behind him in rage and pain. As he watched for it to charge at him, he collected himself and prepared for a second attack. It reeled, wailing in agony. Hot blood poured over Steven's left eye from a cut it had left in his forehead, but it mattered little. He was set on the unknown beast's destruction.

Just before Steven could make his next leap, the shadow grew silent and rose to reveal itself. Before him now stood the form of an unnaturally large being with claws for hands. Steven recognized the beast with a chill. It was the same horrible figure that he'd seen in his nightmare. The witch that had haunted his dream. No other words could describe it. She found him in the night and, for some unknowable reason, she had tried to seduce him with her song in his dream.

Anger swelled in him as he recalled her attempt to lure him in by exposing his fears. This fury brought him to the brink of madness as he glared back at it. With his desire to destroy the witch growing greater than any feeling he'd ever known, Steven prepared for his next attack. It was clear that the witch was bent on killing him and would do so if he didn't fight back.

It turned silently to face him, and he felt a broken tree limb beneath his knee. Steven grasped it with his free hand and rose to meet the witch in defiance.

As he stood still before it in challenge, a low, ungodly growl rumbled through the trees. Lowering his head, his teeth gritted, Steven broke the branch against the ground to give it a sharpened point. Before he could make another move, the creature raced toward him, smashing wildly through the limbs and underbrush. "No!" it roared with the voice of an angered demon.

Gripping his knife tightly, Steven threw the sharpened branch at the charging witch with all his might. It flew through the night and stuck fast into the shadowy head of the beast.

With a screech that loosened the rock on the walls of the canyon above, the witch crashed into an aspen trunk, breaking it off from its base with the force of its charge. The witch wailed and tore at the limb driven into its face. Still clawing wildly at it, the witch leaped up and raced toward the stream in the valley.

With the attack now over, Steven watched in disbelief as the witch disappeared into the shadows of the narrow canyon. Then, he fell onto the soft leaves around him, dazed. The foul odor had been carried away by the breeze and was now replaced with the smell of aspen wood and the freshly upturned earth beneath him. Steven sat in a daydream of exhaustion and disbelief as he waited on the dawn light.

"What the hell just happened?" he thought, unbothered by the blood that now dried on his face. His mind churned for minutes, finding no reasonable answer.

A mule deer caught his attention as it walked amid the suddenly gentle calm of the morning. Unalarmed, it drew a drink from a pool in the nearly empty stream bed. Steven looked up to see another sunny day starting to fall into the canyon along the uppermost rim. He waited for the deer to pass. He didn't want to startle it, as it brought peace to his mind. Soon, it went on its way back down the canyon where he'd come from.

Steven returned to struggling with what he had just encountered and what to do next. He was tired and wondered if everything that had happened that morning was just a dream. But it wasn't. The blood on his face was real.

Easing into a more rational frame of mind, Steven realized he was still gripping his knife so tightly that he could no longer feel his hand. He loosened his grip and noticed the jet-black blood clinging to the blade. It had cut deep, and the blood hadn't dried, unlike his own. Picking up some leaves, he wiped the knife clean and rose to his feet.

Steven walked back up toward the shelter. He found his pack near where he'd struck the witch with it and returned his knife to its sheath, unsure of what to make of the blood. Beneath the pack, there was a shred of filthy, foul-smelling cloth that bore the slash mark of his blade.

He left it where it lay, overwhelmed. His hands began to shake, and he tried desperately to stop them. Feeling weakened, he looked around to make sure he was alone for the breakdown that would inevitably follow.

With a shaking hand, he cleared a few twigs and pebbles from his seat, sat down, and began to weep. Not out of fear, but the utter despair that had become his life. He leaned into his knees and cried until he had no more tears to shed.

After some time, he finally collected himself and stood to pull his pack on once more. Looking in the direction that he'd come, he knew that he could leave this place. He could leave the witch far behind. Then he turned and faced back up the canyon, past where the walls narrowed—back in the direction of the witch's flight.

He would not cry anymore. Or hurt anymore. Or run anymore. He was a broken man that couldn't be pushed any longer, not even by this supernatural being. He would not be driven away by this ungodly beast. There, in the silent majesty of the world around him, he would make his stand, or die trying. A game of life and death. He now lusted for it more than anything. The ultimate mission.

He'd stopped the witch once. Now he was going to kill it.

9

CHAPTER

Chickadees flew down from the branches where they had been catching their morning meals of bugs in the golden leaves. They watched Steven in their curious way as he passed through the aspen forest in pursuit of the witch. The daylight had reached the canyon floor by the time Steven had set off.

Reaching the place where he'd seen the witch disappear, Steven found the same wet black blood on the leaves of the scattered undergrowth. Knowing that he'd inflicted heavy damage with the blade and branch, he was awed by how it could keep moving as it had—almost unfazed.

Its strength was concerning, but his lust to kill it and his delight in hunting again were greater. Although he didn't know exactly what he was dealing with, he knew it bled. And anything that bleeds can die.

The blood trail grew heavier as he found traces of it in the deep-set footprints that the creature left in the sandy soil. He didn't succumb to the faint hope that he might find it lying dead in its tracks ahead, but rather it would be waiting for him like a wounded beast.

Following the blood trail onto the opposite side of the dry stream bed, he found the branch that had been lodged in its face. It was slick with black blood and small pieces of foul, rotting flesh in the noonday sun.

Cautious, Steven began to slow his pursuit, scanning from side to side as he followed the tracks. He would not be taken by surprise if the wounded creature was lying in ambush for him somewhere. He'd learned from being a hunter that both desperate men and animals would often lie to one side of their trail in wait for a passing attacker to pursue them.

By the time the sun started to stretch to unimaginable heights above him, Steven found himself trailing the blood into the narrowest part of the canyon. The aspen grove had stopped, and only a sandy, boulder-strewn landscape lay between the sheer walls.

The narrow box canyon wound back and forth for an unmeasurable distance, cut by the course of the stream at its bottom. Shadows from the steep walls provided some reprieve from the hot afternoon sun. A raven called from far above, and Steven looked up to watch it fly from rim to rim across the bright-blue sky. Before long, the walls began to open back up and provide a view farther up the canyon to where more stands of aspen grew among patches of green grass.

Passing out of the narrow space and entering another aspen glade, the sandy soil and boulders gave way to tall grass mingled among the leaves lying thick on the forest floor. A pleasant and inviting place unfazed by the evil that had passed through it just hours before.

The blood trail became harder to find on the blades of grass and eventually stopped altogether. The impression left in the foliage still gave Steven something to follow. The witch hadn't stopped running since it had fled from him early that morning. Steven guessed that he'd followed it for two miles, and as he'd yet to find a body, he was certain to have the fight he was looking forward to.

Not another soul could be found in this clearing. It was truly a place that man didn't visit. He could see why, knowing now what haunted this place. The tales Mr. Pearson had told about the Indian's warning came flooding back to him. Dismissing the pleasant memories that were intermingled with the tale, Steven remained focused on the hunt.

He pressed on as the afternoon grew late, bathing the canyon in its westering light. Evening was not far off, and the coming night would likely bring another attack. He would again be at a disadvantage in the darkness.

It was obvious that this creature was something supernatural. He'd always dismissed such nonsense as scary stories when he was younger, but as he became a man and saw war, he knew ghosts were real. He'd seen wounded men fighting on without limbs like the walking dead. Shadows of fallen friends had stood next to him in the heat of battle, saving his life with their warnings. Nothing could explain some of the things he'd seen, and after a while, they became as real to him as anything else. There were just some things, both good and evil, that couldn't be explained.

The setting sun finally struck the high rim of the canyon above. Tracking the witch would be impossible in the coming darkness, and Steven needed some cover. He found another good place to shelter for the night. There was only one approach to this position. If the witch came for him, he would be ready this time.

After removing his pack and having a quick meal before the darkness set in, he looked up to see the first stars appearing in the sky. He rested his back against a large boulder at the foot of the canyon wall and began his watch. Though exhausted, he was still alert and focused on surviving and destroying the beast.

The night fell silent, and the long wait until morning began. Steven had found another large limb and sharpened it with his knife as he watched the approach. Time wore on with no sign of the witch. He sat motionless in the darkness of the canyon floor, waiting.

Much to Steven's surprise, the first light of dawn began to chase the stars from the velvety sky overhead. The creature hadn't returned. As the morning started to come alive with birds singing from the treetops above, Steven wondered if he'd wounded the witch worse than he thought. This empowered him; his foe would surely prove easier to finish off once he finally found it.

Waiting until he had enough light to see by, and long before the rays of morning light hit the canyon wall, Steven began to move up the valley again. Pulling his collar up against the morning's cool breeze, he returned to the scattered tracks he'd followed the day before and continued his hunt.

Not long after, he stepped into a grassy area that spread from one canyon wall to the other. It looked almost as if it had once been a pasture, a wide area of exceptionally green grass, where the stream spread out across the flat ground.

Vague as it was, it was the first sign of human activity that he'd seen in the countless miles of broken country. A beautiful and peaceful place, it held an ominous stillness that chilled his soul. The grassy area was deadly silent, without so much as a bird stirring in its whole length.

Steven waded through the tall, thick grass toward the next patch of aspen trees on the upstream side of the large opening ahead. It was again midday, and the blazing sun gave the grass a sweet cinnamon smell as he trod through it. The few tracks that Steven had followed to the edge of this clearing were now lost entirely.

Pausing again in the warmth of the light, Steven couldn't help but be struck by the beauty surrounding him. The emerald-green grass against the bright colors of the rock framing everything around it—the sight seemed like an oasis in the middle of this rather barren place.

He cautiously scanned for any sign of his quarry and noticed the top of a wooden structure over a small rise. He headed in that direction to have a closer look. As he approached, he felt a growing sense that he might finally find his prey hiding there. He stepped out of the grass onto the bare dirt. Before him stood a ramshackle cabin nestled quietly against the base of the canyon wall.

Steven was stricken by the same chill he'd felt when he first saw the witch creeping toward him. He felt an unmistakable presence of evil radiating from within the cabin, and anticipation grew hot within him. He'd found the witch's lair at last.

The cabin was built out of old, weathered timber and still had a shingled roof resting over one half. The door no longer hung in its heavy wood frame. It was lying on the floor amid piles of sand that blew in through the entrance. The cabin's placement near the canyon's wall clearly indicated its builders chose this spot to protect its occupants from the raging elements. A location of necessity rather than choice. Likewise, there was no other place for miles that had signs of abundant water like the lush grass nearby.

No recent evidence of anyone, whether witch or man, could be found in the dirt surrounding the structure. It had clearly not been inhabited by anyone in a long while. It was likely constructed when the state was still a territory. The homesteaders probably wanted to get away from the world—a goal that Steven could well understand.

Feeling safe in the noonday heat, he began to walk slowly toward the doorway. As he approached, a warm breeze turned toward him from the direction of the cabin—along with the strong, foul scent he knew to be his quarry. He no longer wondered where the witch lay, hidden or dead. Steven drew his knife and stopped. He quieted himself to listen for any sign of the creature. The smell of death was overpowering.

As he prepared to step inside, he felt the unevenness of something hard beneath his foot. Next to his worn combat boot was the barrel of a rusted rifle—an old lever-action rifle bearing some harsh scarring on the stock. Sand fell from it as he lifted it to examine the scars further. The damage wasn't wear and tear; the marks were too violent. Knowing the nature of the beast and the stories Mr. Pearson had told, Steven knew the truth. This was the weapon used in a desperate last stand.

Shaking a measure of sorrow from his mind, he stared into the cabin with the glint of revenge in his eyes. He was not a helpless homesteader but a warrior capable of inflicting terror of his own. This cowardly beast had already gotten to taste his fury. Now, he was hell-bent on making it suffer by his hands. The time had come to turn his own demons on it.

Steven set the rusted rifle back where he'd found it, then put his pack beside it. The witch must have known he was there, and since he wasn't attacked the night before, it must have been badly injured.

Steven stepped resolutely onto the weathered doorstep. The timber frame eroded over the years, bleached gray by the sun and pitted by determined insects. Other than the deep piles of sand and debris spread across the floor, the cabin was in fair shape. Although beginning to collapse in some places, the structure's supporting timbers and plank wood covering seemed to be dry and in good condition.

Steven carefully surveyed the interior from the solid footing of the doorway before risking entering the cabin. The warm breeze shifted and drew away the odor of death, for the moment. The canyon remained silent and eerily devoid of bird and beast.

Sunlight poured in through the remaining timber above the half roof. The rest of the roofing lay in pieces on the floor in front of an old hearth. The only piece of furniture that remained was an old table in the middle of the room, partially shaded by the roof that was still intact above it. Everything within the structure was worn from a hundred years of wind and elements. Dust and dirt covered everything in a heavy layer, except where the wind blew strongest through the cracks.

Looking back at the table, Steven spied what looked like a small book resting on it near the hearth. The floorboards creaked as he moved farther into the cabin to have a closer look.

Steven hoped that by entering he might also draw his quarry into the open. But the witch did not seem to be hiding in the dusty room around him. He reasoned that it could only be hidden beneath the floor of the structure, as its telltale smell was still pungent.

Growing more confident in his dire plan, Steven stepped forward cautiously, assessing each step to make sure that he didn't break through the rough-hewn planks. As he approached the table, he saw that the book was a small leather-bound diary. Whatever happened in this place perhaps was chronicled somewhere in its pages.

Steven gripped his knife and looked below him. He was now able to see behind the table, where there was a large hole in the floor along the far wall. It looked as though the floor had been torn open around the cellar door, which was lying in the dust beside it. Sunlight framed the opening through the bare timbers of the roof above it. The daylight still blazed into the cabin from above.

Nothing stirred under the floor. As he reached to pick up the book and put it in his pocket, Steven's roving eyes caught the glint of something along the edge of the cellar opening. There lay a few more drops of the black blood he'd been trailing earlier, still wet after so many hours in the hot sun. Smiling, he was now absolutely certain of where the witch was hiding, if it was still alive.

Knowing that he would have no advantage in entering the cellar, he quickly collected the small book and moved back the way he came. When he reached the solid doorframe, he turned back to have one more look. The chill that had surrounded him before was gone, replaced by a seething sense of anger and fear radiating from the injured witch hiding beneath the floorboards.

He stepped into the dirt outside, and his hair stood on end when he heard the voice of the young woman from his dream coming from below. "Please, don't take it."

Steven quickly turned toward the familiar voice.

"Please, don't take my diary!" it pleaded once more.

Without response, Steven continued to stare at the floor. Nothing moved. Then he heard a young woman singing quietly from beneath the floor. It sounded like a lullaby.

Steven remained fixed against his will, drawn into the moment, recalling his dream. A sense of peace swept over him as the vision of the beautiful woman racing among the shadowed forests rekindled in his mind. Exhaustion began to overcome him, almost as if he were being hypnotized and slowly losing his ambitions. The noon sun seemed to betray Steven, its warmth inviting him into the peaceful daydream. Slowly and without knowing, he stepped back into the doorway, drawn toward the song.

Memories flooded his dizzy head much like they had nights before. He walked through moments of his life, from boyhood to becoming a hardened man. It was as if those memories had never happened. He would be at peace once he held the hand of this enchanting woman.

But the pain that lived with Steven quickly broke his pleasant daydream. He could suddenly recall the betrayal the song ended with and the hatred he'd felt from his weakness.

Realizing the witch was trying to deceive him again, Steven's veins filled with poisonous rage. He snapped out of the enchantment just in time to catch himself in the doorway, about to fall forward onto the floor inside. He scrambled back to the dirt, and the soft voice burst suddenly into anger.

"I will have my diary back," came the witch's cackling voice, "and you will suffer like you never have before!"

The witch raged curses at Steven and pounded on the hidden foundation below. It flailed around in madness over the small diary. With each strike, dust shook from the timbers around the frail structure.

This confirmed Steven's suspicions: the creature couldn't enter the sunlight.

A sinister smile grew on his face. The time for the beast's reckoning had finally arrived. He moved to where he knew the witch could see him and glared intently in its direction. Slowly, Steven pulled the diary from his pocket and began to flip through its pages.

As he did, the witch stopped her mad thrashing beneath the floor. Silence came once more, and dust settled back onto the floor. The old leather binding cracked in his hands, and the witch suddenly roared again in anger.

"No!"

Heavy footfalls came from beneath the floor in front of him as the witch raced to the edge of the light that fell through the cracks below him. Still grinning with smug confidence from his perch in the doorway, he lured the beast closer by holding the diary out where she could see it.

"You want this, don't you?" Steven sneered.

As he peered at the floorboards, he caught the dull glint of a yellow eye glaring back at him. Powerless to collect her book, the witch stood still as death and stared back at him with a hatred so cold that Steven could feel it. As her stifled madness surged, her heavy breathing blew dust up through the crack of the flooring just beyond his feet.

Wanting to drive the witch into further suffering before his plans were fully wrought, Steven began to read from the first page.

"June 9, 1850. We have finally come to the place that Father said we would find to make our home. After the tent was set for the night, Father talked of the house that we will build here and how wonderful it is to have our own land. He said all we need is some hard work, but together we will achieve it. We have come a long way. The travel has been hard, and we lost a few of the cattle that we bought in the last town. But what a beautiful place. It's what an island looks like in the ocean, or so I dream. A lush patch of green life in the middle of nothingness. Father and Mother, as a gift of our new home, gave me this diary and Tommy a rifle. They must have had them hidden in the wagon somewhere."

As he finished the first entry, the beast slammed against the floorboards, causing them to crack. Delighted by the witch's building rage, Steven continued to read through the first few pages of the diary.

The book seemed to chronicle the life of a small homestead family of four as they made a life for themselves and built the cabin. The stories Mr. Pearson had told were true, and now he knew why. He surmised that the cowboy whose cross necklace was found by the Indian guide had certainly met the same fate. The Indians were right to avoid this place. Steven, without question, stood in the very place they called Cross Canyon.

The beast fell silent, looking at him out of the darkened cellar below.

Steven drew a Zippo lighter from is pocket. It bore the emblem of the US Army Rangers on one side. As he flicked the lighter open with its familiar clicking sound, Steven called out, "I don't know who you are, but you're going to burn for what you've done."

A soft growl came from the cellar. Then the broken voice of the creature finally roared at him once more.

"You will know soon. I will drink the blood born of your fear of me! You think that you will live, but you will not. You will be mine. Just like the family and the villagers before them. Just like the men I killed in this cabin. I've been in your dreams. Nothing that you are, nothing that you know, is hidden from me now. You will lie here in this eternal hell with me, Steven. Murderer! It's the least that you deserve!"

Undaunted by the witch perceiving his own mind and weaknesses, Steven scoffed and stared back into the beast's eyes.

"So you think! It is your cowardly blood on the floor, not mine. But take heart as you burn, you piece of shit. For all the blood I've taken, yours will be the last!"

The witch began to cackle, enraging him with its mockery.

"But the blood does not nourish you that you take!," she laughed at him. "You are mortal, and I will make you suffer when the night comes soon." She moved away from the grasping light below. "Read the book if you must. It is ours. A gift from Father before I killed him. The red men couldn't stop me, nor any others. I was here before them all and will be here waiting for the Darkness to come back and reclaim this world of men. Oh yes, my dear boy. You heard what I said. I have been here for an eternity. You cannot destroy me as you desire. I will drink the strength from you as you die in slow agony. There is nothing for you to do now but die!"

Steven's resolve faltered as he struggled to comprehend.

"Look about you, Steven. The night is coming fast, and the daylight will not be able to save you. I will have our diary back soon."

Steven looked up at the deepening sky, then realized the truth in her words. Stepping defiantly onto the timbers of the floor inside the cabin doorway above her, Steven called, "You want this book? Then here it is!"

He tore the small diary in half, and the witch wailed, racing madly back to the edge of the light below. Unwilling to step into even the smallest amount of sunlight, she was unable to reach him, instead clawing in vain at the boards beside his feet.

Stowing half of the diary back in his pocket, he lit his Zippo. He placed the other half of the torn diary into the flame and looked down to see the trapped beast glaring up at him with darkened fury in her yellow eyes. Slowly, Steven fanned the pages into a blaze and looked down to meet the beast's eyes more.

"You may have lived forever," he called, "but you're weak now. I've had your blood on my hands. Enjoy burning in hell!"

And with that, he threw the burning book onto some dry tinder he'd kicked into a pile. The floor above her began to catch fire, and the desperate, unearthly screams of the witch echoed off the canyon walls. She raced to the edge of the daylight and tried to claw at the flooring beneath the burning diary. As her arms passed through the light in the cracks, it burned her flesh, and she reeled back into the darkness.

Steven stepped away from the cabin and laughed loudly enough for her to hear. As the old, dry cabin began to be consumed by the fire, smoke clogged the afternoon air, climbing high toward the canyon's rim and into the blue sky above. Steven's eyes blazed red in the flames as he watched his plan unfold before him. He delighted in the screams of the witch as she burned alive in the fire and daylight.

The heat of the inferno fanned into a whirlwind of destruction as the flames fed greedily upon the aged timbers. Consumed in dark thoughts of his own, it seemed to Steven that the structure itself carried a sense of revenge, doing its part to torture the unwanted beast trapped within its walls.

As the torrent of fire slowly burned its way through the cabin and into the corner where the witch wailed, one last word was heard through the witch's rage. "No!" it screamed in torturous pain, as the flames finally reached her.

In a morbid celebration, Steven began to laugh in earnest—loud enough for the witch to hear him as it burned.

After many long minutes of listening to the hideous struggle below, the witch fell silent. All that could be heard was the sound of flames burning its lair to the ground.

The pungent odor of death was replaced by the purifying smells of burning old pine timbers and the nearby sage lit blaze by the immense heat. It seemed that Steven's mission to destroy the witch was achieved, but he knew better than to walk away before knowing for certain. After the last of the flames turned to embers, Steven walked back to the cabin's smoldering foundation to look for a body.

The roof and some of the floor had collapsed into a dirt cellar below. The floorboards no longer stood over the corner where the witch had been hiding, and the sunlight shone brightly into the opening.

Searching the cellar, Steven couldn't find any trace of the witch, but he knew it was there somewhere in the embers and smoking debris below.

Wanting to be certain, he pulled the remaining half of the diary from his pocket and prepared to burn it. In that moment, the witch burst through a small portion of the intact floor to his right, clawing its way desperately toward him. Steven stepped back out of the cabin as the sunlight scorched her. She wailed. Ripping at her own flesh, she tore herself from the cellar and into the sunlight, casting broken boards to the side with her immense strength.

Steven watched from his position close by as she slowly began to whither in the daylight. Her blackened arms and clawed hands were now visible from beneath a charred cloak and began to smoke in mystical wisps coming from her rotten flesh.

She'd almost fully emerged from the darkness below when she suddenly collapsed onto the timber flooring. Half of her grotesque, cloaked body still hung down into the cellar as the upper half clung with wicked, smoldering claws. Greatly weakened from the fire and the purifying rays of the sun, but still filled with rage, she struggled to pull herself from the hole once more.

Steven had counted on being unable to destroy the witch with fire alone. This foe was great in supernatural ways, but he'd hoped she would be weakened by the fire and the daylight. With her diary in hand, he slowly stepped back to tempt it forward.

Jet-black blood poured from the witch's body and onto the burned wood of the floor. Still trying to reach Steven, she became even weaker with every vain movement. As she crawled through the rays of light, her exposed flesh continued to smoke and cause her torment.

She kept her head veiled with the hood of the singed cloak, while the smoldering flesh of her arms began to fall in sickening masses onto the floor. It was as though the sunlight scorched its bare flesh away from its bones. It would consume her before long.

Watching the witch's struggle begin to come to an end in the light of the Wyoming afternoon sun, Steven stepped toward it again and returned the torn diary back to his pocket. He gripped the rusty rifle from outside the cabin and rested it on one shoulder.

Looming over the dying beast at his feet, he listened to her erratic breathing as her face lay on the smoldering timbers of the floor. Her advance had finally come to an end. Steven scoffed at its weakness.

"I was never afraid of you," Steven said. "And you should have left me alone!"

The witch raised her head from the smoldering floor to reveal its hideous face of sharpened teeth and the yellow eyes of a demon. He felt the young woman he'd heard singing somehow trapped behind those sinister eyes.

Steven felt no mercy for this enemy, like so many before. Without hesitation, he swung the rifle from across his shoulder with both hands and caved in the left side of the witch's face. Blood and flesh poured from the open fracture onto the embers of the smoldering cabin, making wisps of gray smoke as it quenched the heat.

The witch collapsed back onto the floorboards. The claws that had sunk desperately into the wood relaxed, and her lifeless body slipped back into the rubble of the cellar below. Steven heard it land among the dirt and smoldering ashes with a thick thud. He walked to the edge of the opening and looked down to see his conquered enemy's dead body deteriorating in the sunlight.

His mission at an end, Steven threw the rifle down onto the carcass and walked out of the cabin. He'd defeated the witch and would have to fight no longer. It was time to keep moving up the canyon and back into life.

10

CHAPTER

Slinging on his pack, Steven thought about what had just happened. Disbelief had started to sink in. If it all were just a story that he'd heard someone else tell, he would not have believed a word of it. Witches and demons. Feeding on the fears of the innocent. It was all true.

Stories like Mr. Pearson's were accidental warnings passed through generations out of fear, for good reason. And places like that canyon should be left to the unforgiving wildernesses.

As Steven left the cabin behind and made his way up the valley floor into the aspen grove, he recalled similar stories that he'd heard during the war. Stories about ape-men and witches that preyed upon the innocent villagers in the jungles of Vietnam and Cambodia. He no longer doubted those village elders as he once did.

He walked peacefully through the golden glade bathed in the westering sunshine, looking back once more at the smoldering cabin behind him. His nerves began loosening, and he shook from the surge of adrenaline leaving his body. No one would ever believe this story, but it didn't matter. He had no one left to tell.

He was set on being as far from the homestead as possible come nightfall. Not out of fear, but a desire to leave it all behind him, just like the darkness that he ran from back in town. Trying to start over and find some peace of mind would be his objective now.

He thought of the Pearsons again and how he wished he could tell them what had happened. How there would never be a need to fear this place again. He wanted to tell them how he defeated the evil that took so many lives and stained this beautiful place with its poison. But he knew that day would never come. There was no going back. He needed to keep moving toward the new hope that he looked for, away from the troubles that would keep finding him out in the civilized world. He only knew that, for the time being, his salvation would be to hide out in this broken land. Someday, he would have to come back down, but when that would be, he didn't know.

Breathing deeply of the warm Wyoming air, he began to feel relieved of his exhaustion and soreness. After a few hours of walking, his surroundings began to feel clean again. The smoldering cabin was now far behind him. Steven passed from aspen glade to aspen glade and rounded many bends in the valley, the walls of which still rose to great heights on either side of him. Some chickadees flew down to greet him on his passage.

At a clear pool of water in the nearly dry creek bed, he stooped to refill his canteen and took a large drink of water. Its purifying coolness in the calm shade of the day was welcome. He washed the wound on his forehead. Feeling the nightmare wash away with every splash of water on his face, he removed his clothing and slipped into the pool to bathe and scrub his filthy garments.

He lay in the pool, naked and exposed to the world around him, gazing up at the magnificence of the cliffs still dotted with green juniper trees. The sunlight trickled through the falling yellow leaves and into the pool next to him. For a long while, he rested there, feeling a connection between himself and the nature that filled the world around him.

He rose from the water, breaking the stillness as water dripped from his body back into the pool. He stepped back onto the warm, sandy soil of the creek bed and waited until he and his clothing had dried in the sun. Basking in his own vulnerability in this vast land, he felt his place among it. He pondered if all the courses of his life had somehow led him here to a higher purpose. He was sure that he'd at last found his peace.

Feeling rested, and with dry, clean clothes, Steven began on his way again. The first shadows of the box canyon began to creep slowly from the left side to the right as evening set in. The high walls of the canyon shortened as he made his way farther upstream along the creek bed. It looked as though he would soon be reaching the end of this valley, so he pressed on.

It was time to think about looking for his camp for the night. He felt safe enough to have a fire now that he was far away from anyone that might be searching for him. Traveling a little farther into the night than he anticipated, he eventually found a suitable place to stop. Under a velvet sky sparkling with the first stars of evening, he began to make his bed amid a forest floor softened by a thick layer of leaves on the ground. He cleared a spot for a small fire and piled the leaves into a cushion for a bed. Steven hung his pack on a nearby broken branch and went about the business of gathering kindling and wood.

Taking the Zippo lighter from his pocket, he lit the tinder and carefully fanned the flames into the larger bracken. Soon he had a warm fire going, and it lifted his spirits greatly. He gathered some large stones and placed them at the fire's edge to make warming rocks for the cool night ahead.

The firelight made the shadows of the trees dance carelessly through the wood and onto the canyon walls beyond. The night drew in on him as the sky darkened, and the shadows seemed to watch him happily as he settled into his bed for the night. He felt peacefully alone, but that was all right with him.

As he reached to place the coveted lighter deep inside his pocket, his hand brushed against the un-burned half of the diary. A chill swept through his body. He'd intended to throw it into the flames of the cabin once he'd killed the witch but had forgotten. He wondered what more it might tell of the young woman and her family.

He pulled it out and rested it on his knees for closer examination, thumbing at its soft leather edges as he wiped the dust from it.

At first, he was uncertain whether he should read any more of it, but he finally reasoned that he needed to know what had become of the homesteaders and what it said of the witch. He opened it once more and began to read silently among the dancing shadows of the night.

The first several pages told a tale he expected: reports of finishing the cabin and of the pasture being cleared for the few cattle the family possessed. Their life had been meager but happy as they toiled in the rugged valley.

The cellar had been dug by hand out of the rock and sand to keep safe the few vegetables they could grow near a spring that fed into the canyon. The wagon and a team of draft horses had been used to harvest timber from the mountain slopes for the cabin, which the family had intended to expand once the brutality of winter had passed.

Of the few cattle they had, only one could be spared as food for the coming winter. The father and the son, Tom, had supplemented their stores with an elk and a few deer that they hunted at the head of the canyon. By Steven's estimate, that must have been somewhere ahead of him now. It sounded as if just beyond the canyon's head laid a less-broken land, too windswept for their home to survive. Water was not plentiful until one reached the mountain slopes, a day's ride from the valley, so the cabin site in the canyon made a suitable home for the family.

As he read on, Steven began to note the first signs of their happy life unraveling. The family had discovered a small cave hidden in the base of the canyon wall while excavating a pool for the cattle to drink from.

> *July 21, 1881. Father and Tom have be-gun to dig out a trough for the cattle at the spring not far from the house. They have worked for several days to remove a large boulder that seemed to be placed there to block up the cave they discov-ered in the wall behind it. They have found some signs of the Indians mor-taring the boulder to the opening. There they also pulled some oddly shaped stones and feathers from the mouth of the spring. Father said the Indians must have wanted to block it to keep vermin from getting into the source.*

In the chronicle of their winter preparations, Steven read of more misfortunes, even as the diary entries became less frequent.

> *November 20, 1881. It's now late November. The winds never stop blow-ing, and the first snow has fallen in the*

pasture. The cabin keeps away the cold outside, but Father has fallen ill and taken to sleeping most of the day. He forbids us to try and go back to the town doctor, as winter will soon close in on us. He assures us that he will be fine and up and about again soon.

November 28, 1881. Tonight, someone passed through the pasture. Tom couldn't see them in the moonlight on the snow. He called to the stranger, but they ran off. Mother is frightened, as are we all. Father is not well. We pray for help.

December 15, 1881. Tom tried to close the spring once more, as it seems that is where she comes from, but couldn't because the snow was too deep. We cannot sleep now that Father has left us. We can only hope the snow will leave here soon so we can escape this place. She comes every night, and sometimes in my dreams. I'm deathly afraid for our souls.

December 22, 1881. Father was taken from his grave. The demon took him. She has not been back for a week now. We pray the holiness of the yule will save us from her return.

The writing became strange and even more intermittent, almost as if another hand began to pen in the journal.

> *January 1882. Today I awoke in the snow near the cave. I'm afraid of how I got there. Mother and Tom say that I'm ill and need to rest. I cannot sleep. We will never escape this Darkness. I feel sick in my soul and hate myself more than ever. I cannot touch my own skin for fear of the burning cold that never leaves my bones.*

Steven began to wonder more intently about the sinister nature of the events unfolding in the pages before him.

> *I awake in the snow every night. I'm not myself. I'm going to try and leave tonight. I fear myself and the thoughts I have. They are not my own. I am afraid.*
>
> *I have killed Mother. She would not stop screaming when I killed all the animals, even though I begged her to calm. The fear I could smell in her blood made me do it. It has made me feel strong, and I can still taste it. I hate myself. When I can leave this wretched hell of a cabin tonight, I will find Tom after the sun*

*has set, to bring him back. He will not
get far in this deep snow. I will not be
able to write for much longer, as I must
fight whatever I've become to do it. I
need Tom to go on. He will be scared,
but I will need to keep him that way.
God, please save my soul, for I know not
what I've become.*

The following pages were unintelligible, marked by indecipherable words and symbols written by a wicked hand. The final page was blank.

Steven felt the stabbing of fear shoot down his spine as he set the book on one of the stones. It was evident that this family had unearthed the witch that he'd killed, and it was clear now why the beast hadn't killed him in his sleep. It needed him to be afraid.

After whatever she had done to the father, she'd then waited to prey on the rest of the family until there was no longer any hope of them escaping through the deep snows of the Wyoming winter. It had haunted them until it was strong enough to start harvesting them, possessing the daughter during it all.

Steven realized now that fear was the critical source of its strength. It couldn't kill him at first. It had to haunt him. But his resolve was stronger than hers, and his fear had been dulled by all the misery in his life. God only knew what it had done to the daughter.

It was a sad end to a happy family. Steven shook away the chill of the story and once more felt justified in destroying the witch. At the very least, its death may have brought some peace to those poor tortured souls.

Forgetting the words of the diary as best he could, Steven pulled the warming stones around his makeshift bed and lay his head down on a soft pile of extra clothing. As he adjusted the makeshift pillow and pulled his collar up around his neck, he stared warily at the diary.

Unnerved by its presence and the tale contained in its pages, Steven rose from his bed and drew his knife. He walked out among the shadows of the firelight to perform one more task. He picked up the diary and cast it into the edge of the flames, then returned to his bed and quickly drifted off to sleep.

The night fell deep upon his small camp in the aspen grove. As the fire chased away the shadows from the opening where he slept. The small leather book began to smoke. Unheard by Steven, a withered voice far down the canyon screeched in protest.

11

CHAPTER

It was close to the first light of dawn when the fire finally died into a red bed of embers. The diary lay singed but still intact at the edge of the pit. The pungent sweetness of aspen smoke hung heavy in the wood as it cooled in the heavy air. It was the incense giving a feel of holiness to the cathedral of trees.

The calm of the predawn promised another beautiful day to come, and Steven slept on in peace.

As he slept without dreams, a small bird awoke with alarm in a sage bush near the edge of the wood. It flew madly into the silken sky, to the top of the canyon where it could rest once again in safety until the morning light arrived. In the silence of the coming morning, at the base of the same bush, a blackened shape clawed past along the ground.

The witch had come once more.

Though her body was too badly broken to walk, the coming of the night gave her enough strength to wake from the dead. She'd crawled her way through the night to reach him, drawn to her diary and energized by the fear Steven felt while reading it.

With great effort, the witch kept from screeching in pain as she crawled arm by arm through the night. She needed to reserve what little strength she had for the sleeping man.

No longer could she bear down on him with the rage-fueled strength she once had. She had to risk this one last desperate attempt to take him before the shadows left the canyon, or she would fade, unable to escape the hell that haunted her own dreams.

Slowly the dim light of the morning began to brighten the sky and burn away the stars above the rim of the valley walls. The witch's decaying body oozed what little of the black blood she had left, leaving a gleaming trail as she passed. Her hour was finally at hand, and her quarry was near.

Close enough to pounce upon him, she rose silently to her feet with the last of her strength. She drew on the anger and rage she had reserved for this final kill. She needed the man's blood, or she would be no more. The hell that awaited the witch in oblivion was unfathomable, and she feared it all her days. She knew not from where she'd come or when her existence had begun in time immemorial, but she would risk all to keep from falling into that void.

In that last hour before dawn, as Steven lay before her in the wood, her fears consumed her again. Had he chosen to exit the top of the canyon, there would have been no hope for her to take him; she no longer possessed the strength to pass beyond its walls. The stolen body the witch was now trapped in had been badly broken. It quickly drained of the last sickening blood that she'd taken from the men a hundred years prior. This blood had barely kept her from fading into nothingness over the century that had passed. Now, with the last of her demonic strength summoned, it would have to be Steven's blood or the torment of hell that always awaited her.

Desperate, the witch stepped forward to strike. As she did, a limb snapped, loosening a large limb that had been bent back into a trap that Steven had set for her some hours before. The trap sprung and drove the limb across the witch's body, driving dozens of sharpened pegs into her putrid flesh. As she fell back, the trap broke loose from the ground, stuck in her chest and neck. She screeched in pain and fell forward onto her hands and knees as Steven rolled swiftly from his bed and onto his feet.

That very trap had saved his life many times before. He'd been convinced of the witch's death at the cabin, but having read the book in the firelight, he'd begun to think otherwise. Thus, he'd been laying half-awake, suspecting the witch would make one more attempt on his life. Feeling the icy chill from the remaining pages of the diary, he'd figured it might be enough to summon her from her grave. He'd decided to make himself into the bait, drawing her unwittingly into his deadly trap should she come. He knew that she would be even weaker than before, but he also knew that the darkness could work against him.

As he leaped to his feet, Steven produced a spear hidden beneath his bedroll. He plunged it into the wailing beast, driving the weapon through her hobbled back and into the dirt of the forest floor, pinning her helplessly to the ground.

The witch fell silent as she slumped forward, releasing the limb of the trap and grasping the spear that held her to the ground. Steven's blade flashed in the light of the dying fire like the first strokes of the coming dawn. He stood grimly above his victim, running the blade between his forefinger and thumb in anticipation.

Sensing her end at hand, the witch began to weep with the voice of a young woman, and her body seemed to shrink in size before him. She was withering into nothingness before his eyes.

"You never gave your own name in the book. What is it?" Steven looked over his shoulder at the diary lying unburned at the edge of the coals in the fire ring. "If it brings you any comfort, it's going to burn along with you!"

The witch's arms drooped to the ground in surrender. Her weeping stopped.

"You read it," said the witch with the innocent voice of a young woman. "That means you know what I did." She wept once more. "I deserve this."

Steven stared unmoved, with the ravenous eyes of a murderer.

"I killed them all," she said softly as the life in her voice began to leave. "The men on the horses, the boy with his beautiful cross. I hung it at the end of the valley so no one would come here to be taken by her anymore. She tried to stop me, but I could still resist her whenever dawn neared and she grew weak. She'd somehow become me. I never wanted to do all the things that she made me do, but it was as if I could only watch as she used my body for her evil deeds. She is a demon that takes whatever body best suits her witchcraft. Drawing men to her. Like when we came to you in the dream. Men are slowest to fear and quick in their desire to lust. Murdering the strongest makes the weakest fear more easily. You asked me my name. I had almost forgotten that I had one long ago. She wanted me to forget it as I wished for release from this hell that I'm trapped in. My name is Caroline."

At the uttering of her own words, Caroline convulsed and gripped the ground. "I tried to write what happened to me, but it was no longer possible. I remember the night she took me. I was lying in my bed in the corner of the cabin in the darkness, thinking of Father. Somehow she'd gotten into the cellar that night. All I could do was lie helpless in fear as I noticed her in the shadows, rising onto the floor next to me out of the cellar door. I'd never been so scared."

Caroline's hands relaxed as she supported herself on the ground beneath her broken body. She still faced the ground as if in shame and began to sob. "She wore these black robes and stooped over as she neared my bed. I could feel her staring at me from deep within her hood. Then I saw the angry yellow eyes of a cat appear in her shadowed face. I tried to scream. I couldn't even pray for help. My words stuck in my throat from fright. She began to reach for me with these clawed hands."

Caroline lifted a hand from the dirt and stared at it for long moments. It no longer had its wicked, crooked shape but now appeared fleshy and covered in filth.

"That's when I heard the song and I suddenly fell into a dream. I felt myself walking in the warm woods of home once again far from this wretched place. I was not afraid. She was there waiting for me, but not like the wretched beast that I had seen rising from the cellar. She was young and beautiful, and she looked happy to see me. She told me that everything would be all right, and the Darkness would be gone, if I just took her hand. She promised that all would be as it was meant to be, and soon we would no longer be afraid. So, I did. But she lied, or I misunderstood the words. What she meant was that it would be all right for her. She took me so that she could stop the Darkness that she fears most of all: and God's judgment that waits for her beyond it."

Caroline wretched at the uttering of these words and wailed in pain as she tore the ground beneath her.

"Then all I could do was wish for death. I couldn't fight her and tried to run away into the daylight, but I could never get farther than her prison. One by one, I made Mother and the men fear, and I drank it from them. I had to . . . she would not let me go. She must have blood—she made me do it! Please, now is your chance to destroy her. Please destroy us both while you can!"

Steven felt a small measure of sorrow for the woman dying before him. He recalled seeing Caroline in his dream and how she might have lived to be such a beautiful woman in this peaceful land. She was slowly being released from the demon that possessed her, and now he could free her from the wretched prison of her life.

Despite his sorrow for Caroline, he raged even more at the beast inside. It had tortured her into this wretched being. He knew that she was right in her final plea and that he could bring good where evil had flourished for so long. This seemed to be where all the days of his life had led. Through his own dark-ness, he could bring light.

"But do you want to know the worst of it all?" Caroline spoke again, seemingly sensing his thoughts. "I had a brother, Tommy. We were best friends. He tried to protect me as I became this. He would never leave me, even after I fell into this Darkness. After she made me kill Mother, I begged him to run. I let him go for as long as I could. Not to give him a chance to escape, but to make sure that he would keep us alive. He'd feared most of all, you see, and she needed that fear. We dragged him back before dawn. His death did not come quickly, and we consumed him slowly over the days that followed. I guess he will always be a part of us."

To Steven's surprise, she snickered sinisterly.

"Blood born in fear!"

Steven was shocked at her words and wished he didn't feel the remorse and fear that grew in him from hearing them.

Wanting to leave this place as quickly as he could, Steven broke his icy glare and looked up at the first rays of dawn striking the canyon wall.

He looked back down at what now appeared to be a shapely young woman slumped beneath the tattered and filthy cloak.

He took a breath and raised his knife. "I am not afraid of you!"

The witch turned her head to reveal the fair face of the young woman beneath the edge of the hood, a twinkle in her now-blue eyes. "But you are afraid Steven!" The beautiful face of Caroline slowly looked up at him, revealing the side of her head he'd crushed in at the cabin. "You are afraid!" she cackled.

Steven drove his knife down at the witch as she burst from the ground with renewed strength.

As the sunlight slowly crept its way toward the canyon's bottom and began to light the golden tree-tops of the glade, the faint struggle of the man and the witch raged against the stillness of the morning. When the sun had reached the valley floor, the sounds of the desperate struggle between Steven and the witch fell silent. The same bird that had flown to its new perch began to welcome the morning with its song. The day drew on, cool and silent among the majesty of the broken lands and the mountain slopes beyond.

EPILOGUE

Pulling into a freshly constructed parking lot, a couple stepped out of their car and grabbed their backpacks for their long-awaited trek into the Wyoming backcountry.

"I can't believe how far out this place is," the man said to the young woman, placing their final provisions into their packs in preparation for the long hike ahead. He walked around the car to join his partner and took another look back at the town with the Ranger Motel, where they had spent the night at. "We'll have to stop by that general store and do some shopping on the way home. It was pretty cute and looked really rustic."

"Yes," replied the girl, "but this whole state is rustic, so it's not surprising. I think the lady at the motel thought we were crazy for wanting to go hiking up here. Do you believe any of that nonsense that those old guys were saying at the little diner this morning?"

"You mean Cross Canyon and the war hero that disappeared out here years ago? Seemed like they really liked that guy and felt bad for him. But with all that bikers and murder talk, I just think they were trying to scare us back to Denver. Pretty typical out here with these ranchers."

"Well, if they didn't want anybody here, the Bureau of Land Management wouldn't have built these brand-new access lots. Now, can you help me pack so we can get going before it gets any later, please? We only have four days, and if you want to get up to those falls we saw on the map, we need to get moving."

Realizing that she was right, the man busied himself and helped her into her heavy backpack. He locked the car with a confirming beep and slipped the car keys into a pocket on his pack.

He pulled a cell phone from his pocket. "Still no signal."

"Well, duh!" the girl said. "It's Wyoming! And it would be nice if your work didn't call us when we're trying to get away for the weekend."

He held the phone in one hand and placed his arm around her for a photo. "First hike of the year! We'll post that when we get back to the civilized world."

The two backpackers made good time through the hot morning sun. Having no trail to follow, they used a well-defined map that they printed at home. Finding rougher country than they had anticipated, they cut across several small hollows that grew ever deeper as they traversed through the broken lands.

After some hours, they stopped on top of a rocky hill to gaze ahead and take some pictures. From there they were able to plot a more direct course through a valley ahead to the base of the mountain with the falls.

They stopped periodically to drink water and have a light snack before pressing on again through the intense heat. They knew that they would be pressed for time, given their grand plan to hike so far in the four precious days available to them.

The terrain around them was thick with sagebrush and scattered juniper trees and looked like it hadn't changed or been trod by man in many decades. For this they were grateful, as finding untouched wilderness to explore had become increasingly difficult these days. They were cautious to try and stay in more open spaces between bushes and large scattered boulders to avoid an encounter with rattlesnakes in the area, like the one that they saw crushed on the road on the ride to the trailhead.

After some discussion during one of their breaks, they agreed not to press too hard through the day's heat. Their goal of seeing the falls before others started pouring into the newly open tract of public land seemed to be slipping away, given how difficult the surrounding terrain was to traverse in the blazing summer sun. They were content just to be spending time together out in nature again after a long winter working in Colorado's front range.

Before long, the couple reached the valley they had spied from afar. To their pleasant surprise, they found much easier hiking and began to pick up the pace along an old trail carved into the wide valley floor.

After having spent the entire day exposed to the heat, they stopped in the shade of a juniper to reassess their route and current plan of action.

"I didn't count on it being this hot today," stated the girl as she sipped from her canteen.

"Yeah, I know. We're going through water like crazy." The man panted as he wiped the sweat from his brow. "I was sure we would have found some by now based on the satellite imagery."

Pulling the map from his pocket, he found that much of it had been smeared by his sweaty legs. "I got some bad news. Check out the map."

"Well, that's unfortunate! We're not going to find the falls with it now!"

"Let's just cut our losses and hike up one of these canyons to find some water. We can make camp and figure out what we want to do tomorrow. Besides, it's beautiful up in this broken country."

The two of them pressed on up the valley until they could find some sign of flowing water coming from one of the canyons along the side.

After another hour, and almost completely out of water, they came to what they were looking for. The pebbles of the creek bed showed signs of water flowing through recently.

They turned out of the main valley and moved along the bed, passing through glades of aspen, now freshly green from the onset of summer. Eventually the valley floor and walls of the box canyon began to rise sharply above them.

As they went, they marveled at the harsh beauty of the canyon and all the colors of the rock layer high above them. Despite the tall grasses spread out among the aspen groves, the stream showed no signs of water. The heat had been intense during the year, and much of the snowmelt from the mountains above didn't make it far into the land below their base.

After a few more hours of hiking, the first shadows emerged as the sunlight climbed its way up the opposite side of the canyon wall. The coolness that it brought was welcome, but the need for water would soon be dire.

Pausing briefly to consider whether they should push on with the night coming in, they decided to walk a short distance farther. They resolved to not give up the hope of finding some water and thus abandon their hopes of camping here over the long weekend.

Before long, they could see a large patch of green grass where the valley walls opened. They knew that there had to be a spring feeding all that lush grass, and their hopes were rekindled.

As they reached the opening and began walking through the tall grass, both delighted in the feel of it under their feet. Soon they found what they were looking for under a tumbled bank of the dry stream bed: a large pool of fresh water.

Satisfied that they could continue their backpacking adventure for another day, they began to remove their packs and quickly set about filtering water into the empty water bottles. As they worked, the man took note of the lengthening shadows within the canyon.

"Looks like this is as good a place as any to make camp tonight. It's going to be dark soon anyway," he remarked.

The girl concurred with his sound reasoning as they finished filling the last bottle. The couple began to search for a suitable site to set their tent and make a fire before turning in from the exhaustingly hot day. Finding a small patch in the field, they unpacked their light tent and started making preparations for their meal.

"I don't know," the girl said as she looked around while unfurling the tent. "This place is beautiful but seems kind of creepy. And extra quiet."

"I'll keep you safe," the man said with a twinkle in his eye, and she smiled back at him with a reddened face. "I'm going to have a quick look around, then come back and start dinner."

The girl walked into the nearby aspen glade to gather some firewood and tinder as the man began to walk across the lush field of grass in the other direction.

"Watch out for rattlesnakes," she called after him. "They're probably everywhere in this grass."

"I will," he said, smiling about the prospects of the coming night together.

As he stepped through the field, he began to wonder if this had been some sort of old homestead pasture. Soon his suspicions were confirmed, when he spied the top of an old burned-out structure at the base of the deeply shadowed canyon. All at once, he felt an eerie chill on his neck, and the hairs on the back of it stood up.

Shaking himself to his senses, he pressed on toward the remains in the waning evening light.

A raven croaked overhead as it sped down the canyon to its roost on the red rock rim now holding the last rays of the evening sun. It was a warm and pleasant evening, especially after being out hiking in the heat of the day. The air was filled with the cinnamon scent of sweetgrass from the pasture behind him.

Feeling a growing sense of foreboding as he approached the old cabin, the man came to a stop near the old timber doorway near the entrance. Most of it had been badly burned and not much remained of the flooring. He looked back to see if his companion was still visible. The sound of breaking branches and the trace smoke of the small fire she'd built rose over the hill between them. It made him feel better for the moment.

Turning his attention back to the old cabin, he searched the structure from the outside. Just inside the door of the cabin, something strange caught his eye. A small book, torn in half, lay near a large hole in the floor. Upon seeing this, the man couldn't help the fear that welled up inside him.

As he examined the contents of the burned cabin, he began to notice the smell of something dead drifting from inside the structure. This was more than his nerves could stand, and he decided not to get any closer. Nervously looking all around him, he began to withdraw from the edge of the burned doorway. He looked up to see the last light of day leaving the canyon above, and his heart sank.

The man turned to go tell his companion about his sudden change of heart, but he tripped on something protruding from the dirt beneath his feet. Stooping to see what it was, he reached down and lifted a rusty rifle from the burned debris.

As he examined the rifle in the fading light, something else caught his eye. There, atop the dirt, lay a large stained knife with words coarsely scratched into its wooden handle.

He strained to read them in the failing light.
"He feared."

Some beauty should not be tread but left only as a tomb for the ancient dead....

Made in United States
North Haven, CT
22 February 2023

32999724R00114